LUCK

A BILL SHMATA MYSTERY

LUCK

A BILL SHMATA MYSTERY

DAVE CARPENTER

GREAT PLAINS
PUBLICATIONS

Great Plains Publications
420 – 70 Arthur Street
Winnipeg, MB R3B 1G7
www.greatplains.mb.ca

Great Plains Publications gratefully acknowledges the financial support provided for its
publishing program by the Government of Canada through the Book Publishing Industry
Development Program (BPIDP); the Canada Council for the Arts; as well as the Manitoba
Department of Culture, Heritage and Tourism; and the Manitoba Arts Council.

Design & Typography by Relish Design Studio Inc.

Printed in Canada by Kromar Printing Ltd.

CANADIAN CATALOGUING IN PUBLICATION DATA

Main entry under title:

Carpenter, David, 1941-

   Luck / David Carpenter.

   ISBN 1-894283-62-7

   1. Title.

PS8555.A76158L82   2005   C813'.54   C2005-903323-1

FOR BILL KEVER

ACKNOWLEDGEMENTS

I am indebted to members of the Saskatoon Police Service, especially Acting Inspector Lorne Constantinoff and Constable Susan Grant, who answered my questions about operations and procedures with admirable patience. Grant's recent book about the Service, *The Memory Box*, was particularly instructive. I am also indebted to the members of the Saskatoon Coin Club for teaching me more than I ever thought I could learn about scarce coins. I am grateful to Don Kerr, Julie Deimert, Bob Calder, Jake MacDonald, Geoff Ursell, Mark Eisenzimmer and Peter Nash for much help along the way, to the writer David Margoshes for his savagely enthusiastic editing skills, and to Honor Kever, for being my first reader and a whole lot more.

— D.C.

TABLE OF CONTENTS

PROLOGUE: THE BIRD WATCHER   9

PART I: THE SASKATOON CONNECTION
Therapist   13
Your Best Man   20
Coin People   29

PART II: THE LUCK OF THE CLANEYS
The New White Bag   39
Lucky   47
The Visitor   55
Dark   68
Shorty Remembers   72
Bertha's File   82
I Am William Shmata   93
Earl's Pitch   98

PART III: SPRINGTIME IN THE ROCKIES
Tales of Hochelaga   107
Effluent   117
Willie Remembers   122

PART IV: THE DOG
The Pushy Old Man   133
The Stupids   140
Mrs. Miller Tries to Help   144
Julie   148

PART V: SILVER
A Friendly conversation   161
Bertha of the Sorrows   166
Ocean Reconnaisance   174
The Hoard   185
Julie's Luck   191
Joe's Luck   197
The Scorecard   203

PROLOGUE: THE BIRD WATCHER

Saskatoon, August 1951

The crows began to arrive at sunset, gliding over the river in threes and fours, then in dozens, then in vast straggling murders. All through the latter days of August they had been flocking up and roosting in the evergreens and maples surrounding the Sanatorium.

There were fewer tuberculosis patients each year and as time passed, resisting its inevitable demise, the old San had begun to take on the shabby grandeur of a condemned mansion. On two sides of the main building, the outdoor verandas commanded a view of the grounds and seemed to draw the night air into their lungs. The chalets and outbuildings huddled around the main structure among tall pines and lilac bushes, which in turn were surrounded by a scattered maze of willows and weeds that ran down to the river.

Outside the stone and wrought-iron gate that marked the entrance to the grounds, a stately old man stood alone in the dusk. He knew this facility quite well; his wife had passed away at the San, and he liked to imagine her frail spirit hovering over the grounds in summer. It was just an idle form of reminiscence. He had never seen her ghost.

In spite of the failing light, and in spite of a persistent head cold, he was peering through his binoculars at the crows that blackened the dusky sky with their silent passage. So intent was he on the crows, he almost failed to see a small figure make its way across the grass and around the far side of the main building. But the old man's eyesight was still good, and looking up from his binoculars he spotted the figure at the last moment, lugging something and then dragging it behind.

The figure disappeared around the side of the main building. The old man entered by the gate and followed at a safe distance and stood behind a lilac bush. When he spotted the figure again, and this from a distance of more than fifty yards, the person, whoever it was, likely a young boy, was scurrying back and forth, and at last began to hover around one spot.

The old man's attention was diverted by a last great rush of crows coming back across the river. When he peered once more in the direction of the strange figure, he thought he heard a metallic roll from the ground, like stage thunder. Then the figure, the boy, stooped over something on the lawn. The old man had to stifle a sneeze. When he opened his eyes again, the boy was gone.

Had the man felt bold enough to examine the site, had he not been tired and nursing his cold, he would have seen a similar spectacle in reverse. A head emerges, then a torso, then a boy's lean body. It levers itself out of the earth (roll of thunder), and walks, then trots, across the grounds and into the trees.

But the old man had a sleeping child to care for, and he'd promised himself just a five minute stroll. His house was only a block and a half from the San. (He'd moved there to be close to his wife in the final year of her illness.) He returned home with the memory of a boy who simply disappeared into thin air.

He tried to recount what he had just witnessed: first, simply to get the details right, then to assemble them into one of his little anecdotes. As usual, he pretended that his wife was still alive and putting on the kettle for tea. Every event of his life had been recounted to her with yawning frequency, and so this little event, with its night birds and its mysterious young hero, this was definitely something new.

Heavens, she would say, *speak more slowly, Henry. You mean the laddie simply vanished into thin air?*

"My dear," he said out loud, "I mean exactly that!"

PART I: THE SASKATOON CONNECTION

THERAPIST

Vancouver, late February 2003

Bishop Montgomery was ferreting through the elegant detritus of his desk in the study, looking for a spare key for the cleaning lady. He came across a slabbed Edward the Seventh fifty-cent piece from his father's collecting days, as well as his mother's flask for outings in the countryside—which still emitted the faint bloom of brandysoaked leather—and a card bearing his former therapist's name, Claude Gadamer, M.D., F.R.S.P.S. At the very back of the drawer was—*ouch*—a salmon fly; next to the fly, an embossed leatherbound notebook with a tiny gold-plated pen tucked into a leather loop. Bishop withdrew his pricked finger from his mouth.

Absentmindedly he pocketed his father's coin. He checked his watch. It was almost three o'clock.

The gloom of today's rain (as opposed to yesterday's rain or the rain of the day before, *etcetera*) made it seem as though the winter sun was already yawning its way into the Strait of Georgia. No car today, so he would take that nice path to the Tennis Club via Pacific Spirit and Jericho Parks, and just about make it on time for his match.

In spite of his advanced age, Bishop was still able to do workouts and play squash. He had been blessed with good health, a bigboned rugby player's body, and the distinguished facial bones of an aristocrat. Even his thick brown hair seemed to conform to the genetic dictates of a true aristo, and by his seventy-third year, it had turned almost entirely silver. A special silver, he thought, the ninety percent patrician variety that you noticed on the head of his father's Edward the Seventh fifty-cent piece.

Still in mint condition.

Bishop had not amounted to much, he knew that. As a young man he could never quite get his *life going clockwise*, as his father used to say. To placate the old curmudgeon, after a particularly ill-conceived caper, he had accepted a position at a private boys' school in Ontario. Bad luck, that. For more than twenty years he had served as the English master and teams coach, a job that managed to bring out Bishop's bounteous supply of indifference. One week after his father went to his final reward, however, Bishop resigned from the little school in Oakville and, with Mumsy's blessing, probated his father's will. From that moment on, his life began to move clockwise in a pleasant sort of way. He sold the family house in Westmount, purchased his present one in Vancouver, and brought his mother west, where she could grow old in an appropriately waspy environment.

Daddums's little estate.

He had never called him Daddums to his face, and the estate in question had not been little. From the moment his father was in the ground, Bishop had given his energies over to the management of his father's money, and his life unfolded as he had always conceived of it: the gentleman from somewhere else who strode through the world but was not quite of it. Working for a living had been a bit of a bore. Marriage (especially the second one) had been a bit of a bore. But life after marriage, the unencumbered state, had been very much to Bish's liking.

Well, some of the time. Spending the winter in Vancouver's perpetual rain had proven to be not only a bore but probably bad for one's health. Perhaps death itself would be a bore.

Ah, me.

A blue cummerbund from his teaching days, rolled up inside a plastic bag, lay in the most obscure corner of the desk drawer. Beneath the cummerbund, ah yes, was the extra key he would leave for Mrs. Lau. He dropped it into an envelope, penned her a note, enclosed the note and a cheque with the key, licked the envelope and hurriedly thrust the little notepad with the gold-plated pen into the pocket of his workout pants. He snatched up his old cummerbund, held it three feet above the waste basket.

"Up Appleby," he declared. "Fight double blue."

The cummerbund fell into the waste basket without a sound.

On his way out, Bishop dropped the envelope for Mrs. Lau into the mail box, which sat beneath a clutch of dripping ivy, and he set off down Acadia Road at an arthritic but steady clip. A good clip for seventy-two. He was too vain to wear a hat, thought they made him look old, and he'd never gotten the hang of using his umbrella for anything but effect, so he tramped across Northwest Marine, stabbing the ground with his brolly like a London banker, and walked past the wind turbine that spun slowly on the hillside. Soon Bishop had descended an incline to the path he had in mind. Shouldn't take him too long. *Take you a bloody hour*, Spencer had warned, but Spencer tended to over-estimate anything to do with walking. Bishop looked up to his right once again, and now the great wind turbine was riding above the trees, spinning slowly without a sound. There was a sort of android smugness about the thing, with its three-bladed propeller and its ten-story tubular tower and its white silent efficiency. The university engineers had just installed the thing, and everyone on Acadia loathed it.

Bishop checked his watch. Bad form to keep Spencer waiting. Even in retirement, Lamont Spencer comported himself like a corporate cog and had little appreciation or patience for what Bishop referred to as aristo time.

On he went, swinging his brolly. The problem with umbrellas, as Bishop saw it, was that they were made to be forgotten. He had lost a number of them since the move from Montreal, each one black, cheap and undistinguished. One could have retraced his perambulations through the sodden streets of Vancouver over the last decade or two by recovering his lost brollies.

The problem with umbrellas used merely as props, of course, was that you got soaked through to the skin. Van bloody couver. How did these people cope? Bishop had been asking this question for rather a long time. No answers in sight. Bit of a bore, really. He'd been dreaming lately of the Greek Islands, but who the hell went there any more?

The path headed farther into the alders, cedars and densely packed salmonberry bushes and ferns. At last Bishop came to a small wooden bridge over a stream. The path ran parallel to Marine Drive, past Jericho Park, all the way to the Tennis Club.

Maybe Spencer was right. Bishop had been going for ten minutes, he had worked up a sweat, and Jericho Park was nowhere in sight. He was going to tire himself before he even picked up a racquet.

Why, Bishop wondered, did he and Spencer insist on banging that little ball back and forth at their age? Lamont had had arthroscopic surgery on both his knees and he wobbled around like a World War I veteran, and Bish was getting twinges in his hips from osteo-arthritis. Yet they still got dressed in their whites and lurched around the court as if this were normal. Ah, but he was fitter than most men at his age, and he still awakened each morning with a brand new erection.

The rain had seeped through Bishop's walking shoes. As he made his way along the gloomy path, they belched like a pair of large toads. A fine time to take the goddam car in, and like a benevolent fool, he'd left the lender with his daughter Ginny to tool around with. He checked his watch, but it was actually too gloomy to see the numbers on the dial!

He heard the man before he saw him, and then he appeared, treading slowly towards Bishop like a primate who had just learned the joys of vertical motion. He was an old fellow in a convoy coat fastened with wooden pegs, and his gate slackened as soon as he spotted Bishop. As they neared each other, Bishop raised his brolly to be polite.

"Day," he mumbled.

"Bishop Montgomery?" whispered the old fellow.

He had come to a halt in front of Bishop, blocking the path.

"Why, yes."

"Bishy."

The old man's voice was not familiar.

"And you are…"

The old man raised his own umbrella in greeting and brought it thudding down on Bishop's head. Montgomery swayed, stumbled, crashed down on his left shoulder, and became aware that the instrument wielded by the old man had been too heavy for an umbrella. A walking stick perhaps? A putter? He rolled over on his back and looked up at the old man, who was bending down to glare at him: a grey unshaven pale face. The man held a cricket bat, the very sort that Spencer kept in his locker at the Tennis Club. The old fellow leaned down even farther. Bishop could smell the boozy stench of his breath.

Bishop's right arm was free. Still lying in the mud, he swung at the old man's head with his umbrella, the way you might swat a dog. Caught the fellow a good one on the side of his face and he stumbled backwards. Blinked. Held his ground.

"Best you can do, Bishy?"

The problem with cheap umbrellas was their flimsiness. Take a good swing at anything larger than a cat and they cracked somewhere in the middle. Bad luck.

"Why dontcha stand up and gimme another love tap. Hey, Bishypoo?"

He despised that name. His friends had called him that, his enemies, his boys in the upper forms.

16

"Who the goddam hell are you?"

"You don't even know. I was on my way to visit you. Our mutual friend he tole me you'd take this here path, and here you are." The old fellow held his hand up to his mouth as though to impart a joke, but he wasn't grinning.

All at once Bishop thought he might know the fellow, a picture was forming. The awkward way the man had tramped along the path. The high pitch and hoarseness of his voice. The squared-off corners of the man's head, the lantern jaw, the nervous tic of clicking his molars together. The indifferent stare from small jerky eyes. It was starting to come back.

The man's eagerness for violence.

One thing was different, he could see that now. The man had forgotten his place. One could no longer shout him down.

"No need to swing that thing. I'll get up."

Pain was pulsing, tripping through his skull. He tried to gather his strength to stand. He looked up at the man just as he was raising the cricket bat, and down it came whizzing past Bishop's head. Missed by a hair.

"Ya flinched."

The man was laughing now.

"You flinched, Bishy. Now I gotta give you a spankin."

"Yes," said Bish, and smiled bravely, and the smile was not returned, and the bat went up and came down hard on Bishop's right shoulder.

"Please!" Bishop cried out.

"What's my name, asshole?"

"Your name?"

Bishop swallowed, his voice strangled by his own sudden sobbing. He could not remember his assailant's name, not to save his life. His knuckles were bleeding, his father's fifty-cent piece was lying in the mud. He was coming apart.

"Please," he whispered. "Back then, we were just...we weren't even...Can't we just talk about this?"

"Like old times, you mean? Could we mebbe talk about old friendships? Fairness? When I say fairness, what do you think that means, Bishop? Fairness. Does that have some meaning for you? So what is it you'd like to talk about?"

Bishop responded by raising his body up from the wet sand, standing at last, and bawling like a stranded calf. The old man was yelling insane things at him, but he could not stop wailing. Until, at last, the old fellow mentioned Spencer's name.

"What?"

"I said, I just seen our good buddy Lamont Spencer."

The man was shouting in mock glee. The grey unshaven face became terribly animated, eyes blazed with extreme emotion. Was the fellow feeling hurt? Angry over being unappreciated, was that it? No, this was rage.

"Spencer, yknow, he don't look so hot, eh?"

Bishop swayed on the path, clutching his useless umbrella. "He...he..."

"He don't look too good right now, see. Wish you could see him, in the janitor's room there like. Arse in the air? Didn't know them—whutcha call—them racquets went in so far."

"Racquets?"

"Yep. Broke off. Now I'm two outa three, you might say."

"Two out of three?"

At first Bishop had no idea what the man was trying to say, but his head was clearing, and he started to imagine things about broken squash racquets and realized all at once that the man knew exactly what he was talking about. Bishop turned to run back down the path. Something struck him so hard that his body seemed to go one way and his mind the other, and he was on his belly, snorting wet gravel, hearing the profane tirade of the murderer. For now he knew that this man was a murderer, even remembered how he used to misbehave with the girls, it was all coming back, stutteringly, like a film in an old school projector. Bish had even *talked* about this man when he was in therapy. And the stuffed mink, and the card games, and the golf bag. *I must concentrate,* he thought. And still the high-pitched voice of the man raged somewhere above his body in the rain as he kicked him again and again...

...There was a moment or two of buzzing confusion, and pain awakened Bishop once more. He raised his eyelid. The man was gone. The great windmill still turned on the hillside above the forest. All Bishop could hear was the sound of rain dripping off the branches and the periodic splash of tires up on Marine Drive. What was that fellow's name?

I am dying, he told himself. He could no longer feel his feet, his lower legs, his left arm. *Parts of me are dead already. What is left to go?* he wondered. But he remembered the notepad. A last coherent thought in his thundering brain, it had a trace cunning. He took a precious minute to take hold of the notepad, but at last he clutched it in his right hand. He managed to roll over onto his side, insert the pad into his left hand, the one that had no feeling, and he extracted the tiny gold-plated ballpoint from the leather loop with slow intent.

Lungs heaving horribly, he scrawled on the page, one letter, one breath at a time, grammatically fastidious to the end. It felt more like drawing than writing. Capital T...small h...

But now the ghost of his father was yelling at him, I told you, *I told you...get your life running clockwise,* and his watch began to roll backwards and the wind began to rise and sing fragments of an old Bing Crosby song, something about the cool of the evening, and the ocean breakers below were rolling backwards into the sea, even the great windmill, yes, even the windmill had kicked into reverse, even the propeller blades were rolling backwards, even the city with its traffic noises up on Marine Drive, all the vehicles were rolling backwards and now the entire globe had tilted and the sun was gone and the world was plunging backward into darkness, and the younger Bishop became, the louder his father's voice, *Bishop! Bishop, you little two-bit thief, you come back here,* and the louder he yelled the tighter young Bishop clutched his notepad until, in the grip of the counterclockwise planet, he was back there, they were all assembled back there. Right there. Absolutely back.

YOUR BEST MAN

Saskatoon, late February 2003

Mike Letourneau, head of Major Crimes with the Saskatoon Police Service, was reading a faxed report from Vancouver. It had been a long day in a month full of long days for Letourneau (too many investigations, not enough manpower, bickering with the chief, bickering on the home front). It was almost the end of Letourneau's shift, but he had little desire to go home. As police reports go, this was special. It concerned the murder of two wealthy men, lifelong friends apparently, who had been bludgeoned in Vancouver on the same day by a person or persons unknown. Staff Sergeant Letourneau had read many such reports in his life, but rarely were they as lively as this one. He sat by his desk holding a cup of heavily sugared coffee. *First investigator to arrive on scene, Sergeant Colson, noted that vic #1 was found with broken shaft of squash racquet inserted up rectum all the way to the base. Medical examiner concluded this was done after vic was beaten unconscious. Second officer at scene, Sergeant Steel, wonders if assailant had grudge against one or both victims.*

"Sergeant Steel," he muttered, and his massive eyebrows ascended to the creases on his forehead. "Wondered if he had a grudge?" Letourneau's deepbellied laughter erupted, he lost control of his cup, and his coffee exploded like a water bomb on the floor, spraying his socks and shoes.

"Frenchie!" cried Letourneau to the only person on the second floor older than he was, a tall fellow with white curly hair. Frenchie had been custodian of the police station for so long that almost everyone called him Mister Demain. On the day of his retirement, Frenchie had begged to remain on the late shift, so the Department gave him commissionaire status, and after eight more years, he was still there, part of the night cleaning staff. A rumour persisted that the real reason Frenchie had been kept on was that he had an uncanny memory for police work and the lore of the early days.

"Sorry, fella," Letourneau roared. "I just lost it."

Frenchie hauled his bucket over to the scene of the crime, and Letourneau came back to the fax on his desk. *Second vic found on path with notebook in hand, pen in other hand. One word written on page.*

The word was *Therapist*.

The fax included a conjecture or two about the possibility of a mob hit and some sketchy background information. The victim, who had apparently written the word in the notebook just before his death, did not *have a* therapist, or hadn't since his move to Vancouver in the early eighties. Telephone inquiries had been made in Montreal, however, to interview the victim's former therapist.

"Martin goddam Steel."

"Martin Steel, y'say, Mikey?"

The only person alive who could call Letourneau Mikey was Frenchie Demain.

"Remember that young guy? Looked like a college boy? Worked for us up to about 1998?"

"Dark hair? Nice lookin fella?" said Frenchie.

"The same," said Letourneau. "Well, he went to Vancouver with his tail between his legs, and now he's charmin' the pants off the Vancouver Department, looks like. He's already made sergeant. I don't believe it. He wants us to give this top priority, put our best man on the research. Hah."

"Polite fella," Frenchie said, stooping over his mop and pail.

"Detective Steel, yeah. They must think he is some prize." Letourneau glowered at the second page of the fax.

"Mikey, lift your feet. Good, good."

Letourneau rather liked it when Demain called him Mikey. Made him feel young again. The need to feel young again had recently acquired some urgency in Letourneau's life. But not young and stupid. That was Martin Steel's specialty. Steel had come to the Saskatoon Police Service with a B.A. in psychology, highly touted, at a time when the Service was reeling from some bad publicity. Correction: *one* of the times when bad publicity was dogging the force. If the flak from the Milgaard case or the Klassen case or the Stonechild case wasn't enough, there was new flak around the Walter investigation. Some reporters were claiming that Letourneau's boys had been dragging their feet on a case involving the murder of hookers, some of whom were

Aboriginal. And Martin Steel chose that time to grab a tape with some key evidence and play it for his friends just for yucks—and he neglected to bring it back to the station!

It still made Letourneau purple with fury. He turned the page of the faxed report, and in the last paragraph he spotted some words apparently penned by the Vancouver killer and fastened to the body of vic #1: *"Don't Fuck With Saskatoon."* Letourneau read on, the way ardent sports fans follow news about their favourite teams.

Investigator learned from Dr. Gadamer in Montreal that vic #2, found on hiking trail, had once observed crime committed in Saskatoon. Vic #2, according to Dr. Gadamer, had never been able to "put words to this incident," and it remained "buried" during the period of his therapy sessions in Montreal.

Letourneau looked up at Frenchie. It was a long shot, but he gave it a try.

"You ever hear of a crime involving a man named…"

Letourneau squinted at the bottom of the page.

"Bishop Montgomery? Ever hear that name before?"

As two investigators from Major Crimes steered around him, the old man leaned on his mop and stared off into space. Letourneau re-read the last page of the report and when he looked up, Frenchie was still staring into space. So devoted was the old man to the Saskatoon Police Service that he would continue to scan his misty old brain until he keeled over from exhaustion.

"Never mind," said Letourneau.

The report concluded with a request for information from the Saskatoon Police. *Montgomery (vic #2) had no known enemies in Vancouver or Montreal. Request search of trial transcripts for information re: investigations involving said vic #2 or re: concerning said vic #1, Lamont Spencer.*

"Yeah, why not? We got nothin better to do out here." Letourneau rubbed his eyes. "No enemies in Vancouver or Montreal, hey? How in the sweet Jesus do you know that? That is vintage Martin Steel. He lets somebody else do his dirty work. And I wouldn't be surprised if he wrote this fax."

"Well well," said Frenchie.

"Yer damn rights. But he knows that if he signs the goddam thing he might not get his precious information."

"Didn't sign the fax, eh. Well well."

Frenchie drained his mop, picked up his pail and trudged out the door. Letourneau got one of the gals to run the name *Montgomery, Bishop* on her *CPIC* program. He waited for a moment, and she drew a zero. He returned to his own desk, and when he looked up, Frenchie was back, still holding the pail.

"Say that name again, Mikey?"

"What name?"

"The whatzit, you know."

Letourneau checked his screen.

"Bishop Montgomery."

"Wasn't he the witness for that drowning?"

Letourneau squinted at the old man.

"In the river," said Frenchie. "Off the bridge. The guy got throwed off the bridge."

"You remember that from fifty years ago?"

"The guy that got drownded, he lived in our neighbourhood. Guy had a golf bag?"

"My God, what a memory," said Letourneau.

"Throwed the bag in the river too. Didn't find no body, didn't find no golf bag."

Letourneau was smiling.

"Frenchie, give me the name of the victim and you can run this goddam department."

"Joe Claney," said the old man. "Ran a bit wild, eh. Had some scrapes with the law. I knew the fella, knew his family."

Over the past decade in Saskatoon, it had become apparent that the beleaguered Police Service needed to keep better records, and to preserve these records for future investigations, inquiries and posterity. To this end, the Saskatoon Police Service had hired its own librarian, a researcher by the name of Bertha Eeling. In early January, she was seconded for two years on a trial basis from the Local History Room of the Public Library to work on files for a police archives, which became known as *The Annals of the Saskatoon Police*. Bertha saw a book at the end of all this, but when her zeal to write it became known, she was urged to confine her research to the older records and avoid writing about recent high-profile cases that might some day return to haunt the Service.

In the first week of her new post she was given access to all of the police files from 1902 to 1977. She could do write-ups on anything that might come under the broad category of Human Interest. The archive would some day be open to the public, so nothing could be admitted that might discredit current members of the force, or compromise the security of an active investigation. In her second year, Bertha was told, she might be allowed to work on more recent documents.

Once in a while Mike Letourneau would consult with Bertha on files that needed to be reactivated, and it looked as though the sad chronicle of Joseph Claney would be one of those. Claney had apparently stolen some money from some hotel employees. He had stuffed it all into a golf bag and returned home to Saskatoon. He was tracked down by the men he'd stolen from (who had learned of his whereabouts from a man who had driven Claney to the train), and one of them had thrown Claney off the CPR Bridge. One of Frenchie's sources for this information was Joe Claney's younger brother, who by now might very well be pushing up daisies.

The Claney story had been deemed fair play for Bertha Eeling, and she wrote it up for the Archives. But this afternoon, with the fax about the two murders in Vancouver, Letourneau decided to reactivate the file. This decision gave him a nice excuse to visit Bertha in her basement lair. It was a bright little glassed-in office surrounded by gloomy acres of metal shelves stacked with records. Her office looked like a diner in a garbage dump.

"Bertha, darlin!" he called.

Bertha Eeling peered warily over the rims of her glasses.

"I need our file on the Claney case, 1951 or '52."

"Oh dear," she muttered.

"Oh dear?"

"You mean the Bulger file, don't you."

"Whatever."

"I was mulling it over last month. I wanted to do more research on the people involved. Expand it a bit more."

"No harm in that, Bertha. Except that file is now part of an investigation. You got it handy?"

"It's at home," she said. "I can bring it in tomorrow."

"You take this stuff home with you?"

"Of course," she said. "Sometimes that's the only way I can get anything written up."

Bertha paused and softened her voice somewhat. "Mike, I don't suppose I could keep on working with the file...um...while you worked with it up there?"

"Not a good idea. Not now anyways."

"Well," she said with some regret, "goodbye, Mr. Claney."

"Be a sweetheart, Bertha, and give it to the research clerk upstairs?" He gestured towards the dark rows of stacks outside her basement office. "God, Bertha, this is gloomy down here."

"I like it just fine," she said. "It suits me."

"Do all librarians love to live like moles?"

"Just the dedicated ones," said Bertha.

Letourneau left her little hovel for the stacks, humming the Lara theme from *Doctor Zhivago*.

"Where's the goddam light switch down here?" he cried, his voice thundering through the stacks.

Bertha said nothing in reply, but a moment later, the stacks were flooded with light.

"Thank you, Bertha."

He just wanted to look at them for a moment, all those files from as far back as 1902, before Saskatchewan had even become a province. Row upon dark row of closed cases, cold cases, court reports, records that no one cared about any more. Except for Bertha. She was slowly becoming the Police Service's memory. She and Frenchie Demain.

"You know your way around all this stuff?" he called.

"I'm beginning to," she replied from her office.

"Thank God somebody does."

Letourneau began to regret telling Bertha that she shouldn't pursue her Claney research to expand the file. Little harm could come of it, and Bertha's research was exhaustive. But if the chief found out that a librarian was assisting in an active investigation, there would be shit to pay. Still, it wasn't an active file until Letourneau said it was. Technically.

He returned to Bertha's office. She was reading something in a very Bertha-like pose: eyes close to the page, glasses drooping well down on the nose. Crow's feet around the eyes. How in hell, on a fifty-year-old woman, could that way of reading a file be so fetching? He could watch her read like that for hours.

"Bertha?"

She peered up.

"Look, you wanna keep goin with the Claney file on the Q.T., that's aces with me. Just copy our stuff and give us the originals."

"Bless you, Mike," she said and gave him a smile.

A smile from Bertha went a long way with Letourneau. He had to pull himself away from the entrance to her office. He had just done a no-no. He had just given her the nod to carry on with a file that was probably going to get activated. Was he getting the stupids? To put it more honestly, was Letourneau getting the stupids over Bertha? What other stupid things had he been doing?

Out went the lights in the stacks.

The job at hand reclaimed his attention. The problem with the Claney query sent by Steel in Vancouver (he was sure it was Steel, the little suck), was that the Saskatoon Police Service had no choice in the matter. They had to co-operate, because if Letourneau needed information from the Vancouver Department on a case, he knew he could count on the Vancouver people to supply it. These days police services all had to count on each other.

But because of budgetary restraints, the Saskatoon Service was once again understaffed. Letourneau would have to put a man on Steel's request for information and transcripts. Even with the help of Bertha's file, that man might spend several days hunting up all the relevant details instead of working on active cases in Saskatoon where he was needed. And this week alone in Saskatoon they were investigating a kidnapping, a hit and run, a home invasion and two different goddam homicides.

"Wait a minute…"

"Are you still there?" Bertha called out.

"Bertha?"

Letourneau strode out of the gloom of the stacks and up to the bright little office once again.

"Just one question. I've been talking about the Claney investigation with Frenchie upstairs. He actually knew the guy who got killed. Why do you think they never found Claney's body or any of the money?"

Bertha allowed herself a smug little smile.

"Because," she said, "the South Saskatchewan River was in flood, and he was swept under. And because the golf bag with the booty inside was filled…with…"

Bertha's hands beckoned a reply from Letourneau.

"Gold bricks?"

"Silver dollars."

"Was there a brother?"

"There was indeed. Joe's younger brother Earl."

"So, Frenchie was right. And this brother, he's still—"

"He was on my list of interviewees," said Bertha. "I've turned up a few things on the man. You can see my notes if you want."

Letourneau waved away her suggestion.

"No notes, Bertha. Just this Earl's last-known and the stuff you've already typed up. Let's keep things simple."

He turned to go.

"Did you know that Earl Claney used to phone the Service?" she said.

"No kiddin."

"Apparently, in his cups, he used to phone up the Service and ask for a Detective Salter. Years after Salter had retired, he would still ask for him. Once he filed a complaint about the delays in the investigation. They had arrested the fellow who did the murder, he got a life sentence, but apparently Earl thought there was more to it than that."

"Life for a crime with no body?" said Letourneau.

"You'll have to read my notes," said Bertha. Then she put up her hand, "I know, later." Her attention was once more reclaimed by her work.

Letourneau lumbered up the stairs to the main floor of the building, thinking about a golf bag filled with silver dollars. He knew now where to take this thing. Not to his superior, who would bitch about manpower shortages. Not to one of his own men in Major Crimes, and certainly not back to Bertha. The way to go was his friend Bill Shmata, who was crazy about old coins. He had retired early from the Police Service for health reasons, but Shmata was used on an ad hoc basis by Major Crimes to do bits of digging around. They could use him to look into cold cases as long as Shmata called upon the Police Service to lay any charges or make arrests, and as long as the Service could justify paying him, piece-meal, out of their stingy budget.

Once in a while, if he felt like it, Shmata did work for free. And right now he owed Letourneau. He might not want to take this bit of work. He might even get resentful over doing the Service's digging for them, unless Letourneau could dress this up a bit. Make it into a challenge for his former colleague.

Letourneau ambled out into the parking lot for a smoke and watched a city worker cleave through the new snow with a small grader. He lit up in the cold air and his watchful mug went slowly sardonic. *So, Detective Steel, you want my best man for the job?*

Letourneau inhaled enough smoke to fill an oxygen tent. He pulled out a cell phone, keyed in a number. He was thinking once again about the silver dollars in the golf bag.

"Hello?" said a familiar voice.

"Hello, you old sad sack, how are you?"

"As miserable as ever," said the voice.

"Keeping busy?"

"Much too busy," the voice replied.

"Too bad, buddy," said Letourneau. "I think I've got a job for you."

COIN PEOPLE

Saskatoon, late February 2003

Bill Shmata was perched on a hard and unforgiving chair. As the meeting droned on, he was forced to shift his buttocks from left to right and back again. Shmata was seated next to his old friend Daniel Meiers, president of the Saskatoon Numismatic Society. Meiers had finally convinced Shmata to join the club. What the hell, it was less awkward than AA meetings. A room full of coin people, about thirty of them tonight, and only one or two wearing any outward signs of wealth. A friendly bunch, by and large. They paid close attention to Daniel, the owner of a coin store on Broadway, and Shmata's friend from the seventies when Shmata had been a cop on the beat. The club members were clearly tolerant of Daniel's jokes, his fussiness, and his pedantic enthusiasm for the minutiae of coin collecting.

"Now, don't…do not…pick up a Victorian fifty-cent piece like it was a cookie. Pick it up by the rim and keep your fingerprints to yourself. Like Ham is doing. Eeee-yes."

This evening Daniel was showing them how to grade Victorian, Edwardian, and George V half-dollars. He had assembled a kit with all the distinguishing features for every grade of coin from heavily worn to uncirculated. He passed around some samples of fifty-cent pieces in a range of grades from his own inventory.

"Remember," he reminded them, "this is an exam, and the best way to fail is to over-grade your coins. Think of these as *your* coins and think of me as a prospective buyer."

"Lemme get this straight," said the old fellow who was holding the fifty-cent piece. "You want me to think of these coins as mine?"

A sarcastic smile from Daniel.

"No, Ham. Mine all mine."

"You got any *twenny-ones* in this pile?" said another fellow.

"Very funny," said Daniel.

Shmata made a mental note to ask Daniel what was so special about a twenny-one. He was becoming well-versed in American pennies and American silver dollars, but he knew next to nothing about Canadian coins.

The grading session went on for almost an hour before Daniel called a break in the proceedings. At last Shmata was able to stand up and ease his aching buttocks. The big old fellow made a beeline for Shmata and held out his hand.

"Ham Walmsley," he said. "I've been away from the meetings for quite a long time. Say, don't I know you from the papers?"

Bill Shmata raised his finger to his lips, and whispered at the old fellow, "I would appreciate not being identified here by my old trade."

The fellow looked down, nodded abruptly, and gave Shmata a complicit wrinkle of his forehead.

"I'm not here as an investigator," Shmata said, continuing to whisper. "You understand, I'm just here to learn, like the rest of you."

"I understand," said Walmsley. "I understand completely. But I'm not here to learn."

"No?"

"Not me, no. I'm returning to the club this year so that I can accumulate a great sparkling pirate's chest full of gold and silver to roll around in before I die."

Shmata chuckled.

"Have you retired from the police?" said Walmsley.

"More or less," said Shmata with a weary frown. "Daniel seems to think I need a hobby, so I guess this is it."

Shmata had indeed retired from the Saskatoon Police Service, for reasons of health, but in the past few years, as he made his way into his sixties, he'd been doing a fair bit of investigative work on contract and hoping that, eventually, the Service would take him back part-time. He had just sent them a letter to this effect. The City of Saskatoon had licensed him as a Special Investigator, which meant that he could receive small stipends to beef up his disability income. Once in a while, when Shmata had successfully wrapped up an inquiry, there was some reward money or insurance payouts to be had, but lately these trickles of income had dwindled.

"Well," said Walmsley, devoid of any irony, "it's a good hobby. The hobby of kings, or so they say." Walmsley looked down at the tiles of the meeting room floor for a moment and then looked up at Shmata. "What do you want to collect?" he asked.

"I heard that gentleman over there refer to *twenny-ones*," said Shmata. "Maybe I'll go for some of them."

Daniel Meiers interrupted them.

"Bill, Ham, coffee's ready."

They made their way around the circle of chairs and past the samples of ungraded fifty-cent pieces, Walmsley following Shmata close behind. Shmata picked up a coffee and a donut and turned to Walmsley.

"By the way," said Shmata, "what are twenty-ones?"

"Hah!" said Walmsley, as they strolled back to their chairs. The man clearly thought Shmata was joking.

Meiers had placed his coins in his briefcase. He and Shmata were heading for the doorway, when it was suddenly darkened by the large and ominous form of Staff Sergeant Mike Letourneau. He was wearing a massive new blue parka with a great ring of animal hair around the hood and holding an unlit cigarette with the usual question on his lips.

"What are you doing here?" said Shmata.

"I been hawkin louies and I thought I'd show you a few. Can I, ah…"

"No, Mike," said Shmata. "Outside."

They drove to Bork's, where Letourneau could smoke and Shmata could sip tea without feeling conspicuous among all the beer drinkers. Whatever you drank at Bork's, there seemed to be an atmosphere of permission. There they sat: Shmata, small in stature, softspoken, precise, guardedly hopeful on good days, the gent who always asked the questions; and the big cop Letourneau, who answered them with a booming voice, cynicism and suspicion always just below the surface. Letourneau had brought a file that he'd been perusing, and he pushed it halfway across the table in Shmata's direction.

"Can't get useta seein you with a cup a tea."

"Work on it, Mike."

"I'll work on my beer," he muttered, glowering at a table of young bohemians situated between them and the front door. He had never been easy on university students.

"Anyway," Letourneau continued, "I can't get you a contract this time."

"Why not?"

"It's the goddam city. The accounting department is whining about double dipping. It's suddenly a big thing with them."

"So," said Shmata, "you want me to do some digging into this Earl Claney's past."

"Right."

Letourneau began to fill Shmata in on the details of the Vancouver case and the Saskatoon connection.

"Last thing the vic did before he croaked was write down a word. *Therapist.* And since his days in Montreal, he never *had* a therapist. Can you beat that?"

"Therapist," said Shmata. "Just that one word?"

Letourneau nodded. He had just come from reading the file, he said, and found out that Earl Claney was still alive. But for some reason, he wanted to dump the file on Shmata as soon as possible.

"And the city isn't giving me a contract. Well, Mike, a good boy scout is not supposed to say this, but who pays me?"

"It's just a bit of checking around, Bill. Trial transcripts and stuff—"

"You want me to work for free."

"Shmata, how much work have I brought your way over the last few years, eh? It's just this once. I got a feeling about this one. I think this might turn into something."

Shmata sat up on his sore buttocks. "You want me to dig into this old fellow's past and what? Harrass him a bit? Find out if he still carries a grudge?"

"No," said Letourneau, and a familiar snarl returned to his voice. "Stay the fuck away from Claney. Who knows, he might turn out to be our guy, so we don't want him to know we're lookin into things. Not yet. Do some snooping, but don't go near him unless you talk to me first." Letourneau smiled playfully at his friend. "Besides, Shmata, he's not that old. Earl Claney is just a few years older than you are. Guys your age should show some respect for each other."

Shmata muttered an oath at the floor. "The other day at the Safeway," he said, "the girl at the till, young girl, she asked me if I was a senior. Said there was a discount for seniors."

"And?"

"I pretended I was sixty-five. I saved five bucks."

"Your point being?"

"I'm not used to people assuming I'm a senior. I tell her yes, I'm an old fart, I save five bucks, she says, *Do you want some help out with your groceries?* Jeez."

"Shmata, they say that to everybody."

"They never used to say that to me."

"Shmata, read my lips. They say that to everybody. They have to. It's P fuckin R."

"How would you know, Letourneau? You've never bought groceries in your entire life."

"I get groceries for Francie, okay? And they always say, *Sir, can you use some fuckin help.*"

Letourneau leaned over and placed his big hand on the file across the table. He seemed about to open up on something.

"What is this?" said Shmata. "Why should I do this?"

Letourneau shrugged. "I got a hunch about this one."

"This case is a Letourneau hunch, then? Why don't you put a man on it?"

"No can do, Shmata. You read the papers? Major Crimes is up to its arsehole in kidnappings, murders and all kinds of other shit. Some investigators in Vancouver just need some information. I can't put a man on a job like this just to answer a goddam fax for another goddam police service."

"So, basically, I'm poking around for free, reading trial transcripts or whatever so that you can answer a fax from another police service."

"Shmata, there's stuff here. Interesting stuff. Questions to be answered. This guy Earl Claney, I swear he is the key to somethin here. He useta phone us at the Service about his brother's murder. Back when you were walkin a beat. He was phonin us years after they sent that other guy up for murder."

"The one who—"

"The one who tossed Joe Claney off the bridge. Years after his brother's murder, Claney was some pissed off. If we're lookin for motive for those two high livers in Vancouver, this guy Claney's got motive up the wazoo."

"But they caught his brother's murderer."

Letourneau nodded. "Yeah, they caught the right guy, too. Sent him away for life. Just made a phonecall and I found out that he's dead. I forget his name. It's all in the file."

"You don't even remember the assailant's name? And…and how could he possibly get life when they never even found the body?"

Letourneau was glowering at the bohemians again. He turned back to face Shmata and leaned forward on his elbows. "Take it easy, Shmata. Jesus, you were more fun when you were a drunk. I think his name was Bolger." Letourneau rubbed his eyes with the palms of his hands. A sort of weariness appeared to have over-taken him. "Look," he said, "it's been a kind of up and down month. I been up and down about a lotta things. You gonna do this or not?"

"You've been up and down about what?"

"Things," he said with a rueful smile. "I think the job is gettin to me. Lately I been gettin the stupids. I mean the job is the job. I can handle it, I got it covered. But the stupids, that's somethin else."

"The stupids?"

There was no answer. Letourneau was gazing off into the smoky reaches of the bar and grinning warily. At times when he went vague like this on Shmata, he often said *I got it covered.* Repeated it compulsively. Shmata left his friend alone. If Letourneau wanted to spout off, he would do it. But it was clear to Shmata that something in Letourneau's life was getting to him. Maybe burnout. Or maybe he'd been breaking the rules. Shmata was not particularly big on true confessions among friends.

"Look," said Letourneau at last, "I could maybe get some money for you. It wouldn't be much, but I could justify using you as a resource. You know, like an informant? We've actually got some money in the informant budget."

"So, if I take this file, poke around, and find a connection between Earl Claney and these two dead guys in Vancouver, you'll pick this guy up?"

"A possibility."

"You know what I'd really like, Letourneau, is a chance to come back part-time. Any chance of that?"

Letourneau shrugged. "I could ask around. You do this Vancouver thing for me, I'll see what I can do for you."

Tempted though he was, Shmata remained noncommittal. "To the investigators in Vancouver," he said, "this is an active case. So I'd be working on an active case. How would you square that with your superintendent?"

"There could be a problem," said Letourneau, "frinstance if you tried to take the guy in yourself. But to us, officially, this is just info to the boys in Vancouver. I don't expect no trouble, and if there's any flak, I'll take it."

"So I read the file, check out the details of this murder trial fifty years ago, and then…. Why not talk with Earl Claney?"

"No. Leave him for one of my guys."

"I don't know, Mike. I don't have much latitude to *do* anything here."

Letourneau flashed a cunning smile. He was tapping the file nervously, with both hands.

"Shmata, did I tell you about the golf bag?"

"What golf bag?"

"I thought I told you," Letourneau mumbled around an unlit cigarette, putting down the file again, rifling his pockets for his lighter. "Gal who worked up the file for me, a mad keen researcher named Bertha Eeling, she filled me in on some of the details. Her and Frenchie."

Good old Frenchie.

"The golf bag," Letourneau continued, "Bertha tells me that it was filled with money. You can check the details with Bertha. But that's what they were fightin over. A golf bag filled to the brim with goddam silver dollars. Find them dollars, you might just open a few doors."

Shmata stared at his friend. "You're shitting me."

"Shmata, you're a coin collecting nut, so I brought this thing to you. I got a hunch about it, and no way can I justify putting one of our guys on it. Not with how we're stretched right now. But I am not shitting you. See for yourself. It's in the goddam file. You take this little bit of digging around, Bill me boy, you'll find yourself on a goddam treasure hunt."

Shmata smiled suspiciously at his friend, but behind his sardonic facade, Shmata began to wonder, and questions began to emerge, and the questions begat more questions. A golf bag full of silver dollars. Plunging into the river fifty-two years ago. Would coins like these register on a metal detector under water?

Wouldn't they oxidize out of all recognition and be worthless? What would hotel employees be doing with a big hoard of silver dollars? Where would they have come from?

"Well?" said Letourneau.

Shmata looked up.

"Huh?"

"Where the hell have you been?"

"Nineteen fifty-one," said Shmata, reaching at last for the file.

PART II: LUCK OF THE CLANEYS

THE NEW WHITE BAG

Montreal, May 1951

After a good deal of pacing, Elwood Montgomery was once more hunched over at his desk in the big study, wondering what a good father should say to his son at the moment of departure. Young Bishop would soon be boarding a train for Banff and—who knows—perhaps leaving Montreal forever. Elwood tapped his long fingers on the blotter that covered part of his desk. *Well, Bishy, don't forget to write to your old dad now and then. Well, Bishy, your mother and I will be thinking of you, never far from our thoughts, you know. Well, Bishy, old son, a word to the wise: do remember the benefits of the old French letter. Well, Bishop, I have no idea why you'd want to do another summer in the bloody mountains when you could be out in the world with a real job, making your own decisions, YOUR OWN INCOME.*

Elwood Montgomery, Chauncey to his friends, was a tall man with a waggish yet almost regal bearing. His family had always lived in Mount Royal and affected a Britishness so imperious and stodgy that it could be mistaken for caricature. More English than the English, everyone said. In his study, glowering beneath the mounted heads of two whitetails (Tim Buck and Tim Buck Two), Chauncey looked like a country gentleman from practically any era.

He had a great drooping moustache that appeared to be cultivated for size and comic effect, a head of silver curls and expressive clumpy grey eyebrows that slanted downwards, lending dignity and shade to his perpetually watery eyes. When he had enjoyed a gin too many, or when, like now, he was beset by unreasonable demands, his features seemed to droop and crinkle like old dollar bills.

Well, Bishy, old top, I must admit, I don't know a hell of a lot about your life, and the less I know the happier I'll be, but for the love of God, man, you're twenty-one years old…and…

Chauncey groaned out loud. He had some sorting to do before his son came home, and he knew he shouldn't put it off much longer. The Westmount Numismatic Society was meeting tonight, and besides, it wouldn't do to flaunt the family hoard in front of his spendthrift son. His debauched gadabout wastrel soon-to-be-leaving son.

Perhaps he should have a drink.

Chauncey's wife Jane was back in England with her sister, swapping disapproving stories about men and gadding about while he held the fort in Mount Royal. Mrs. McNabb (Nabbers to the Montgomerys) would be his housekeeper until the duration. Nabbers's daughter (delightful girl with a fetching little gap between her upper front teeth and a roguish laugh) would not return to her usual duties assisting her mother until Jane Montgomery had returned from her stay in England. In other words, Chauncey had been left without any temptations.

He and young Bishop were on their own for several weeks. The boy had apparently decided to become a layabout for the rest of his life. His main preoccupations now were racquet sports, cards and boozing. He had broken up with his girlfriend, whatsername, Suzie from the club. The silly bugger had sent her up the stump, and it had had to be dealt with. Chauncey had played the role of Pitiless Pater in this little drama because Jane had decided to retire to her chamber until the storm had blown over. Bad show all around.

Now that university classes were over, instead of getting a job, young Bishop had decided to return to the mountains with his friend, Spencer, to be a bellboy at the Hochelaga once again. The lad simply had no rudder. What was it now, their fourth summer there? And to think, it was Chauncey and Jocko Spencer who had twisted the appropriate arms to get the boys their jobs at the Hochelaga in the first place.

Jane had always spoiled Bishop, but Chauncey, well, he was a man after all, he had responsibilities at the distillery, and he had never really spent much time with his son. Now Chauncey and Jane were reaping the benefits of too much coddling and too little discipline. Chauncey was inches away from compelling the boy to sign up with the old regiment heading out for Korea. Give him some spine, remind him what the world was about.

Oh, Jane would love that.

And if young Bishop weren't enough to worry about, Chauncey's position with the distillery was becoming a bit of a bore. He had brought his family name to the business and a nice bit of lolly to get them started, and they had always retained him as a vice president to charm the moneyed classes and promote the product. Then they had gone public, and now they had a bloody board of directors, which meant too many tedious meetings, too much fuss and bother with new accounts and new accounting practices and roll-forwards, whatever they were, and soon they would have Chauncey flogging the booze all across the country like some Fuller Brush man. Altogether too much like work.

This was the gentleman's great tragedy, especially since the war: if you wanted to hang onto the family jewels, you had to go and work at a bloody profession. There was some money to be made out there now, signs of prosperity. Building rows and rows of those appalling little bungalows like Jocko Spencer was doing, or mucking around in the oil patch in Alberta or some equally depressing place. Building highways from nowhere to nowhere.

Thoughts like these made Chauncey feel his age. In fact, he was a very lively sixty, he could still put away his share of G & Ts, he could still enjoy some randy pleasures with the odd office girl here, the odd housekeeper there. But he was a late starter in the marriage business, and consequently he was too old to have a layabout son to worry about. And goddam it, on this beautiful May weekend, socked in by his gloomy musings, banging around through the great house, he was feeling old.

Well, Bishy, there you go. Off to the mountains for a last lark before the big crunch of reality, hm?

The only place in the great house in which Chauncey felt comfortable was the den where he kept his coins and his flask. He could lock the door, slide the false panel in his walk-in closet, open the big safe, and haul out the canvas bags heavy with the coins he had been acquiring since boyhood, the mint rolls and numismatic proof sets, the English gold sovereigns and twenty dollar St. Gaudens gold pieces, the pouches of loose change from his own father's ragtag collection, and loveliest of all, the newly struck silver dollars that he had been acquiring annually from the mints, the American banks and the ones downtown in Montreal. Alone with his coins in the study, his flask full of Pinch, Chauncey became someone else entirely.

He stooped over to look into the safe, pawed around to find the right bags, and lifted them out for culling and separating.

Today, because he was gloomy, it would be silver dollars. There was nothing like silver dollars to bring back the colour to a man's cheeks. Still hunched over, he emerged from the safe with a large bag in each hand and set them down on his desk with two great clunks. He brought out two more bags and plunked them down as well. He was always surprised at the great heft of them. The four old grey bags were made of tough canvas and bore the logos of the Bank of Montreal, the Bank of Nova Scotia, the Bank of America, and the Royal Canadian Mint.

Chauncey found a sturdy canvas bag with a drawstring on the top shelf of the safe. It was folded in half, pristine and white, with black lettering: *Retourner à Monnaie Royale Canadienne.* He placed this bag on his desk and upended one of the older ones. The coins tumbled out over his desk blotter. Almost half the bulk of these coins was fifty-cent pieces, which he had heedlessly tossed in with the silver dollars. He picked them out of the pile and dropped them into the white bag by the handful. Expensive now, these half dollars, the early ones getting hard to find. Victorians from 1870 on, King Edwards, George the Fifths, all in mint condition, some of them a bit pricey, but smaller than the dollars, less clunky, and therefore less inclined to bring out the pirate in Chauncey. One of the half dollars was in a plastic slab, a lovely 1905 Edward, and he stuck it into his pants pocket to deal with later. He didn't like them slabbed or placed in holders of any kind. He liked to be able to pick up a coin by the rim and tilt it up to the light.

The fellows at the Numismatic Society said he was crazy, that all his good coins should be enclosed to protect them against wear and smudging, but Chauncey was not a numismatist. He wasn't fussy enough. He didn't want to *study* coins, he didn't want to imprison them in cardboard folders or plastic. He just wanted to *acquire* them. The problem, however, was that he had now acquired too many and they had to be sorted. Rare and expensive ones in the new white bag, common dates back in the old bags. These latter he would take down to the coin club tonight and trade the lot of them for just a few of the tougher ones to find. Didn't want to end up cornering the market on silver.

Hurry, Chauncey, hurry up.

What remained on the large green blotter on his desk was an impressive pile of Canadian silver dollars, most of them frosty white and lustrous. They had been purchased, year by year, at the bank downtown and originally had come wrapped in paper rolls or individual cardboard holders, but now they lay on the blotter as free as fish in a stream. They might get a bit marked up from time to time, but after all, these were just dollars. They had only cost a dollar, so why not enjoy them?

Some day, he had been told, these beauties would shoot up in value like the earlier fifty-cent pieces had. Limited number of strikes and all that. So even if one's love for the coins was entirely boyish, one could also think of them as an extension of one's portfolio, and they were a lot more fun than Canada Savings Bonds or blue chip stocks.

Chauncey began to stack his dollars in piles according to date. He poured out another bagful, this one with no half dollars mixed in, and the little piles on his desk blotter began to grow. Lots of 1935s, lots of 1936s, fewer 1937s, and only seven 1938s. When he came to the 1948s, he discovered that he had only four of them. Hadn't the collections fellow told him that this was the toughest year? Yes, a snafu at the Mint or something like that. He said collectors were buying them up these days for thirty dollars apiece. Chauncey had to browbeat the man just to acquire these four. By contrast, his stack of 1949s with the lovely ship on the reverse was so high that he had to make three columns, and many of those coins were just pocket change.

Chauncey was so absorbed by his stacks of silver dollars, and lulled by the first nip or two from his flask, that he had forgotten the imminence of his son's departure. He gathered together all the 1938s, 1945s, 1947s and 1948s from among the small pillars of silver before him and placed these scarcer ones in the pristine white bag with the pricey half dollars. He returned the rest of the Canadian dollars into their two bags, put them in the safe, and returned to upend two larger bags of American silver dollars. Some of the Peace dollars were just as white and flashy as the Canadian ones but some of the Morgan dollars, because they were older, were heavily toned in opulent shades of green and purple, pale gold and magenta. The miracle of oxidation. Cartwheels, they called them. Surely some of these beauties would be worth a bit of lolly. He began to stack them according to year and mintmark, the way a fussy old fellow at the numismatic club had shown him. He looked up at the window to his study and saw that the late afternoon light was bright and beckoning. He ought to go for a walk and get a bit of exercise. Hell with it. It was Sunday. He could do what he liked. He would stack coins till midnight if he wanted to.

An hour later the entire surface of his desk was covered with short and tall stacks of US dollars. The lovely Morgans with Miss Liberty on the obverse and the beautiful eagle on the reverse: they started on Chauncey's far left at 1878, and ended on the right edge of the desk at 1921. The Peace dollars were arranged above the Morgans, and they went from 1921 to 1935. They were less exciting to look at. The Liberty gal and the eagle were less well struck, less intricate, and who exactly was a *Peace* dollar supposed to impress?

"Bolshies and nancy boys, that's who," he said out loud, glaring up at Tim Buck and his friend.

Still, among the Peace dollars, there seemed to be a pattern emerging here on the blotter. Only two 1928s and two 1921s. Chauncey tucked them away in the new white bag.

He picked over the Morgan dollars with more enthusiasm and care, and he was cheered in his labours by a few sips (well, a few gulps) from the flask of Pinch. Low tally of Carson City Morgans, an oversupply of New Orleans dollars. Another tug on the flask. Relatively few San Francisco dollars, and a big supply of Philly ones. Tiny stacks of any coins around 1893 to 1895. And so it went until the flask was empty and the new white bag was bulging. He arose from his desk, swayed for a moment, and looped the draw-string over one of Tim Buck's antlers. The sorted coins swung back and forth in the gloomy light like a bag of suet.

Chauncey heard the front door close with an authoritative *whump*, and he was up and running. He began to scoop up handfuls of dollars until all the common dates were back in the two older bags. Chauncey teetered with a bag in each hand and made for the safe. He put them inside next to the Canadian dollars and slammed the door of the safe, spun the dial, slid back the oak panel. Scuttling back from his labours, he heard his son singing as he clambered up the first flight of stairs from the foyer, *Bloody Mary is the girl I love...bum bum bum bum...*

Chauncey unlocked the door to his study, swaying from the effects of the sudden exertion and the scotch.

Young Bishop thumped once on Chauncey's door, opened it, poked his head inside, and a great waft of beer and cigarettes floated into the room. He gazed past his father's face and into the study.

"Hallo, Pater. Guarding the castle, I see?"

"Hello yourself, son. You have been drinking."

"Nonsense. Did you like my singing?"

Chauncey frowned at the boy and wondered if he had forgotten something.

"I could switch songs if you liked. Bit of the old Bing, perhaps?"

"Bugger off."

Young Bishop crooned a few lines from *In the Cool Cool Cool of the Evening*.

"If you persist in this concert, my boy, I shall have you sent to sing among the *castratis*."

"Father, I'm going to be a bit short until I get paid at the hotel. Could you float me a couple of hundred?"

Chauncey reached into his pocket, felt the slabbed Edward, and dug deeper into his roll of bills. He could not bring himself to hand over the money.

"You know, Bishy, you're going to have to get a job."

"Yes, Father."

"I mean, young man, when you finish there in August. You've just got to go out and work for a living. Find out a few things about the world. Live on your own for a while."

The young man heaved a histrionic sigh.

"I mean, we can't keep subsidizing your boozing and gambling forever, son, can we? I mean, there's got to be a moment—"

"Please, Father, no sermons. This is just to tide me over till pay day. I mean, I might want to eat supper or something decadent like that over the next few weeks."

"You always seem to have enough money to get yourself squiffed."

"Squiffed?"

"You know what I mean."

Chauncey was still fingering his roll of bills. He was no nearer to bringing them out.

"Isn't it just possible, Bishy, that if I give you less money, you might just do less drinking? Fewer all night poker games? Hm?"

He pulled out the roll, pealed off two twenties and a ten, pocketed the rest, and handed over the money.

"Food for thought, Bishop."

Without counting them, the young man folded the bills, bowed to his father and ran up the stairs to his room on the third floor.

Well, Chauncey, he put it to himself, *that wasn't so bad, was it? Father and son part on good terms, eh? Son a bit the wiser, Pater a bit the richer?*

Exhaling scotch and patriarchal righteousness, he went downstairs, roamed the big house for a while, and at last lay down on the chesterfield in the library. He closed his eyes and went right out. He woke up briefly when he heard some rattling at the front door. *Bye-bye, Bishy.* Son had made his own arrangements to get a ride to the train. He was gone for the summer. Chauncey closed his eyes again. He had just about fallen back to sleep when it occurred to him what he had forgotten to do.

LUCKY

Southern Alberta, May 1951

Joe Claney was getting a special feeling, maybe something to do with the motion of the train, which murmured *Hochelaga, Hochelaga, Hochelaga* as it clattered across the prairies. The feeling also had something to do with a song by Mario Lanza that he could not boot out of his brain, and maybe something to do with feeling like Houdini, his hero, the guy with the tricks, and a lot to do with the beers he'd been putting away all afternoon in the club car, and, yes, something to do with winning at poker. Ever since he switched trains in Regina and headed west for Calgary, his luck had begun to soar. He rifled through his pillow case and counted up his booty. Fifty-seven bucks, a brass pocket watch, a jacknife, a stuffed weasel, a two-thirds full mickey of Walker's Special Old, and a brand new silver dollar.

Joe had wedged himself into the can to comb his hair. He thrust his happy mug up closer to the mirror. A dark slit had opened up in the centre of his lower lip. He could taste his own blood. Little scrap he'd had with a guy in Saskatoon who owed him money. Damn. He'd have to remember to smoke out of the corner of his mouth and not get into any beefs until the thing had healed. He winked at himself. He smiled. *So kiss a me my sweet, eetsa da loveliest night of the year.*

Ever since Claney had quit school four years ago, he had bumped along from job to job, always looking for the fast bill and dogged by lousy luck. The trouble with fast bills was that they went in and out of your wallet faster than shit through a goose. It was time for a change. It was time for Joe Claney to come up in the world. He dabbed with a hanky at the blood on his lip.

He kept gazing at his reflection as he combed his pompadour, worked it back into its original crouch. It hurt to smile, so he smirked into the mirror. Like the stuffed weasel in his pillow case. *Hochelaga, Hochelaga, Hochelaga.* He put away his comb and hauled out his pecker and pissed a bucketful.

The more he thought about the present situation, the hornier he got. There were some gorgeous broads on this train. He'd love to bump into one of them and see if she was in the mood. *Comeon a my house, Baby...*

Sing it, Rosey.

Joe Claney was in the mood. He was a yard dog ready to howl. He was making tracks out of Saskatoon, disappearing like the Great Houdini, he was on a train stuffed with wild fillies heading for the mountains, he couldn't lose at poker, he would never again have to listen to his mother and his gramma tell him to get off his ass.

He zipped up and lurched out of the can, pillowcase over his shoulder, breathing beer from every pore. *Hochelaga, Hochelaga, choo choo choo...*

The fellas were still assembled in the club car and they gave him the Bronx cheer as he shuffled toward them. Joe's place at the tables had been taken by some bigtime operator who looked like a movie star. He had a movie star tan the colour of rich person shit. Claney was about to tell the bozo to move on, but something made him stop. The fellow looked up.

"Well," he said, "you must be the *lucky* one."

"Yeah?" Joe replied. "Howdja guess?"

"I don't see anyone else in here with a pillow case full of money. Do you?"

The movie star held out his hand. On a bad day, Joe might of conked the guy right there, he looked like a real a wise ass, but instead, he shook the fellow's hand. Guy had a grip like a bench vise.

"Bishop Montgomery," said the fellow.

"I'm Joe Claney."

Bishop Montgomery was headed for Banff, he confided. Almost everyone in the train, he told Claney, was headed for summer jobs in Banff and Lake Louise.

"Lamont," the fellow said, tapping another prince on the shoulder. "I want you to meet Joe Claney."

The new guy held out his hand, a real gent.

"Lamont Spencer," he said. Crunch.

The movie star, Montgomery, raised his hand and beckoned to the coloured guy at the bar.

LUCK

"Waiter?"

The waiter gave Montgomery the once-over, like he couldn't believe a high roller like this would travel with the peasants.

"A beer for me, my good man, another for my friend, and one for Mr. Claney. Thank you."

Claney couldn't be *that* drunk. Something was going on here. These two swells were hustling him. But why would two guys who looked like godddam royalty be hustling Joe Claney?

Oh, yeah. He remembered, today he was lucky. They sensed it in him, they were drawn to it. When you had it, luck, that is, people flocked to you. The broads and the swells and everyone. So instead of lipping off to the two princes (one was Spencer, one was Montgomery, he had to remember so they wouldn't think he was stupid), he just let things drift. He smiled, licked some blood off his lip, squeezed into another chair, and decided he would enjoy the ride. The beers arrived and Bishop Montgomery paid for them.

Joe couldn't keep his eyes off these two. Lamont Spencer, a natty look about him, with his perfectly clipped fingernails and his tight little smiles and hearty laugh and a tight little curl combed over his forehead. Bishop Montgomery, with the sleepy blinkers and the bored look of a matinee idol. You could tell, they had the world by the tail and all the tail in the world. Bell-boys, they were both going to be bellboys! They called themselves *bellmen*. Joe had never heard that word before.

He had blundered into a movie set, and someone must have given him a part to play but they'd forgotten to hand him a script, and he was all eyes to discover how this one was supposed to end. Who got the girl here? (There were more and more, hotel chars and waitresses and laundry gals, buzzing around their table.) Who walked off with the big prize? Who got shafted? Who ended up doing time?

Joe Claney's job, when he left the train in Banff, would be in the kitchen of the Hochelaga, washing dishes on an assembly line with a legion of working stiffs from the wrong side of the tracks. But who knew that at this stage of the ride? For all anyone in the train knew, he might be the jeezly tennis pro.

After a few drinks he was fast friends with these fellows. Cards? Yeah, he could manage a few hands. They stood up from the tables, went through a couple of sleeping cars, and the girls were everywhere, gabbing with their friends, bare legs hanging out of the upper berths.

"Holy Joe!" cried one of the girls, and Claney turned his head, but she and her two friends were gawking at Montgomery, trying to catch his eye.

"Simply utterly!"

"Hey, Bishy-poo!"

"Swooo-ny!"

Claney wanted to be simply utterly and swoony. Another beer might help.

"Goom bye!" called one of the girls.

"Goom bye," Claney called back.

He followed Spencer into a different lounge car and sat down at the largest booth. This car was for people who had entire rooms and roomettes and liked to stretch out. People who were rollin, in other words. A club car with a kapital K. He met another bunch of 'bellmen' bound for the Hochelaga and did another round of wincing handshakes. Did all these guys have a Charles Atlas type grip?

The only guy he wasn't particularly drawn to was a short fellow named Willie who kept his eyes on Spencer as though he were waiting for orders. Swiss Willie, someone called him. He kept real quiet, maybe he was just off the boat. When they were all seated around the largest booth, it was announced that this Willie character would be the Bank. He was in charge of the chips.

And the chips—Claney had never seen this before—the chips were not wood or plastic, they were silver halves and goddam silver dollars. A *tradition*, Spencer said.

Joe bought fifty dollars worth of silver.

Minimum bet, fifty cents and fifty cents to ante up. Bishop Montgomery hauled out his own precious pile of cash from a suitcase on the floor, a nice white canvas bag bulging with coins. Some of the coins were Yankee dollars, and because they belonged to this Bishop character, they seemed to have more flash than all the others. If you didn't have your own coins, you bought them from Swiss Willie. He would take in the cash and dole out the guys' chips from a big Seagram's bag, and he scarcely spoke loud enough for Claney to hear him.

Another guy showed up, a bellman from down east named Buckler, and from his jacket he dragged out a leather pouch full of coins.

"Dealer's choice?" asked Spencer.

"Dealer's choice," agreed Montgomery.

"Five card stud for starters." said Spencer.

"Five card it is," said Montgomery.

"Everyone bet on the second card," said Spencer.

"Second card-o-reeno," said Montgomery.

"Everyone ante up." said Spencer.

"Ya-ya," said the Swiss guy.

Five guys at a card table, the biggest booth in the club car. Up came a waitress bound for Banff, tight skirt, short cropped hair and a great body. She lit up a smoke and looked on. She was joined by a couple of Hochelaga chars who loved to crack their chewing gum like a pair of crickets, and a hotel nursing assistant named Lottie, cute little blonde who smiled a lot and couldn't speak much English. Cripes, the classiest pussy he had ever seen. Joe Claney tilted his beer, took a mighty swallow, and the train chugged across the prairies for Calgary. He was in heaven. He was becoming simply utterly. He tossed a shiny silver fifty-cent piece into the pot.

"Luck a the Irish," he said.

Another fellow wandered in, moody looking guy, somewhat older than the rest of them. Flat-top, spooky eyes, looked like a World War II vet. He loomed over the table, checked out a few hands.

"Want in, old top?" asked Spencer.

"Maybe later," said the fellow, and ordered a beer.

The next time Joe Claney looked up, the soldier boy and the blonde nursing assistant, they were walking away from the table.

"He says he vants me took his picture," the blonde girl said.

As the two left, the others hooted, and the train blew its whistle as though in response.

"How on earth," said Spencer, "did that speciman get a job as a bellman?"

"You mean Bulger?" said Montgomery. "Our new manager is an egalitarian."

"I'll see you," said Spencer, "and raise you five."

Claney peeked at his cards one more time, a pair of jacks and a pair of fives, king high. He smiled for the boys, the patented Houdini smile, resigned and worldweary, equal parts bitterness and merriment, because after twenty years on the earth, he still didn't know how the story ended. He licked his lip and tasted blood.

"I'm callin you guys," Claney said, and moved a small pile of silver into the pot.

The Swiss guy, Silent Willie, was looking distracted. He was gazing at the exit where the big guy named Bulger and the blonde nurse named Lottie had gone through.

Lamont Spencer peered over his glasses and smiled at Claney, which gave the effect of one pair of eyes on Claney's face, the other on his hand. Spencer laid down a pair of aces and a pair of queens.

"Tough luck, old boy."

Spencer raked in the silver, and kept raking it in, until, all at once, they heard somebody scream in the next car. Everyone stared, then Bishop Montgomery went to investigate. Another guy took the deal and Claney won a hand. Claney took the deal and won again. Spencer took the deal and delayed, waiting for Montgomery, shaking his head. *Bloody Bulger*, Spencer kept muttering.

"Who?" said Claney.

"Nothing."

What is goin' on here?

At last Montgomery returned, whispered something about the women's can into Spencer's ear. Spencer dealt a hand of blackjack and dropped fifty to Buckler, then Montgomery took the deal again and Spencer won a bundle. From that point on, Montgomery and Spencer kept raking in the moola, and Claney lost or had to fold almost every hand. There was something funny about this setup, but he couldn't tell how they'd rigged it. Claney had boarded the train in Saskatoon with sixty-five bucks. He had won fifty-seven more in the other club car. When he stood up from the card table, he wasn't sure if he even had enough for a meal. His head was spinning and someone was trying to talk to him.

"What, are you on the shorts?" said Spencer. "What else do you have in that pillowcase, old boy?"

"Nothin you'd be interested in, *old boy*."

"Let's have a peek, Claney. Just a peek?"

Joe sat down again and hauled out the booty from his afternoon winning streak with the working stiffs in the other club car. He placed each object on the table, the mickey of rye (ooh), the jacknife *(hoya hoya hoya)*, the silver dollar *(ahhh)*, the pocket watch *(ooh la la)*, and at last he came to the stuffed animal and placed it on the table.

"Claney," said Spencer, "what in the name of God is that?"

"It's nothin. It's just a stuffed weasel."

Montgomery picked it up and brought it to his nose. They glared at each other for a moment, rodent and bellman.

"That, Claney, is a mink. And a prime specimen at that."

"Old Bishy-poo knows his mink all right," cried the fellow named Buckler.

So Claney played a few more hands until all he was left with was some change and the empty pillow case, which he draped over his head so he could pretend that he had disappeared. Some Houdini. He stood up from the table.

"Goom bye," he hollered.

"Goom bye," they hollered back.

Claney found himself lurching away from seat to seat, passing from car to car, hoping to get as far from all these well-heeled assholes as he could go, and he bumped into the older guy, the soldier boy named Bulger, who recoiled like a cobra—*sorry sorry*—and Soldier Boy lurched past, looking just as drunk as Claney was, and finally, Claney made his way to the end of the next car. When he tried the door, all he could see was a hundred miles of track and dusky prairie receding into the east like a bad memory.

"This is the caboose," someone said.

Two young women were sitting deep in conversation. One of them was snivelling and her face was red and glistening with tears.

"End of the line," said one of them. "Far as you can go."

He sat down on a long, wide faded purple seat across from the two young women. He recognized them from the card game. The snivelling one with the red face was the little blonde nursing assistant, some kind of D.P., and the one who did the talking was the waitress with the great body. Her name was Suzie. They were hunched over on a small bunk facing Joe.

"Nice train," he said. "Nice view like."

"You weren't about to jump off, were you?"

"No, hell. Just wanna see the view."

A brakeman came in, smiled at the two young women, picked up a clipboard and went out again.

Claney looked at the blonde one, hip to hip with her friend on the seat.

"You havin a bad ride?" he said to her.

"Hah," she laughed, tearfully.

"Scuse me, Miss, but I couldn't help notice that you was in a bad way. If you want, I could go and leave you girls be."

"Oh," said her friend, Suzie the waitress, "Lottie's feeling a little bit blue, aren't you Lottie."

"Ya," said Lottie. "Liddle bit blue."

"You can stay," said Suzie. "The brakeman says it's okay if we stay here. I just don't want anybody bothering Lottie, you understand?"

Claney did not have a clue what she was getting at, but they made him feel like a bodyguard or a fellow orphan or something, it was better by far than hanging out at a crooked poker game, so he stayed with the girls in the caboose, and all the way to Calgary and beyond to the mountains, the three of them talked, and slept, and woke again and talked through the night.

THE VISITOR

Saskatoon, February to early March 2003

"Fella come by to see you, Earl."

"Y'don't say."

"Never left his name, but I'd be worried if I was you."

"Probly one a my rich relatives wants to leave me their life savins."

"Oh, I don't know, Earl. This guy looked like a bill collector."

"Ha."

Earl Claney was living at Mrs. Miller's place, known to the outside world as Supreme Home Care. He was sitting on the back patio, bundled up in his parka, having a smoke with Julie Belanger, one of the women who worked for Mrs. Miller. The snow piled up around the patio was beginning to melt. The sun felt good on his face. He hadn't felt warmth like that for months.

"He just come up here when I was on my walk?" Earl asked Julie. "Didn't leave no name, just took off?"

Julie shrugged her narrow shoulders. She was a blackhaired Métis woman many years Earl's junior. Talking with Julie and smoking on the patio seemed to be the only two consolations for living at Supreme Home Care.

When they brought Earl to live here, he had told no one. He was ashamed to tell his friends. Revealing his whereabouts in a dump like this would be like telling his drinking buddies that he was in prison. Did prisoners really want folks to visit them in all their shame and dejection? No thanks, not for Earl Claney. But maybe, somehow, word had travelled.

By most people's reckoning, Mrs. Miller's establishment was not considered to be a dump. It had the only trees of any size on the crescent. The food was okay, better by far than the swill Earl consumed in the beverage room of the King Edward. During honest moments when Earl was not quite so dis-spirited about things, he could admit that Supreme Home Care was not such a bad deal for seniors who could afford it. Not bad for old ladies. Earl was the only man at Mrs. Miller's, and younger than any of the other guests by at least ten years.

"Sure that feller wasn't a cop?" Earl whispered to Julie.

"He told me his name!"

A voice was blaring from inside the kitchen window, the megaphonic strains of Mrs. Miller, a short, stacked firehydrant of a woman who could yell loud enough to rattle the windows of any house. She went on the assumption that all of her charges were hard of hearing (which Earl was not), and had seemingly forgotten how to speak at normal volume. Earl sat up and craned his scrawny neck back towards the house.

"Funny kinda name," Mrs. Miller bellowed through the window. "Can't for the life of me remember…"

"Was it about the house?" Earl shouted, screwed around like a tom turkey checking for predators. No response.

Earlier in February the cops had phoned Claney to tell him that his house had been broken into. Then again, maybe this mysterious caller was a doctor bearing bad news for Earl. Did doctors make housecalls to places like Mrs. Miller's?

"So-so height," boomed Mrs. Miller's voice. At this moment she would be standing in front of the kitchen sink, washing pots. "About your age or younger, Mr. Claney. Funny name."

"Probably a bill collector," said Julie, who never shouted at anyone. She stood, squinting at the melting snow, and stubbed out her cigarette in the tin can they both kept on the patio. "Comin to get you, Earl. Jig's up for you."

Old neighbourhoods in Saskatoon look uniquely and eccentrically Saskatonian. They sprawl along the streets that conform to the bends of the river, working class neighbourhoods lined with colourful clutters of old frame houses, or blueblood crescents on the wealthy side of town: old stone and brick wonders, terraced gardens and long docks reaching out into the river.

Brand new neighbourhoods in Saskatoon strive for that look of bright-eyed prosperity, little miracles of positive thinking that manage to look like thousands of other brand new neighbourhoods up and down the continent. Earl Claney had been moved from the first kind of neighbourhood (the working class version) to the second kind, a heavily mortgaged community known as Vista Lake. He'd been a widower since 1993, and retired from his cabinet making busines since 1999. His entire social life had descended into one corner of the beverage room of the King Edward Hotel. The move to Vista Lake had come suddenly. He had been suffering from nausea and headaches. On the advice of his doctor, he had tried giving up on drinking and smoking for an entire month, but the new regime seemed to make no difference. If anything, his binge of abstention had made him feel worse.

While raking leaves in his front yard one day, Earl had blacked out with a seizure. His neighbours picked Earl up and took him to Emergency. Hauling him had not been as difficult as one might have imagined; since the headaches had begun he had gone down in weight to about one hundred and twenty-five pounds. They kept him at the hospital for a full battery of tests, including x-rays of his bones, gastro-intestinal tract, skull and lungs. After a CT scan, an MRI and an EEG, his doctor told Earl that he had a brain tumor. To make matters worse, it had come from some other cancer in his body, a mother lode of malignancy that all their tests could not locate. They sent him to a neuro-surgeon who had a go at the tumor. It had grown large enough to increase the pressure inside Earl's skull and cause not only the headaches and nausea, but the seizure as well.

The neurosurgeon, a self-possessed young physician from Iran, managed to excise most of the tumor. The remaining portion was inoperable, so the staff at the cancer clinic zapped it for two months and sent Earl off to try and live out his life as long as the cancer would allow.

Because he had some money socked away, and because he asked not to be put into a nursing home, they sent him to Mrs. Miller's place in Vista Lake. Supreme Home Care was a big sprawling new bungalow, a private care home for seniors who weren't far enough gone to be shipped off to nursing homes. In every room of the house the décor was relentlessly cheerful, but in those same rooms, a dark and tacit assumption hovered like smog: no one would ever leave Mrs. Miller's home alive.

Each of Mrs. Miller's guests was given a private bedroom. All the food was prepared in her kitchen, and the ladies would toddle into her breakfast nook for their meals. Earl always sat in the chair by the back door leading out to Mrs. Miller's patio. After each meal he could excuse himself from the ladies and, in a flash, be smoking in a favourite deck chair, bundled up in his parka and his gloom.

Perhaps Earl's cancer was in remission. Perhaps he was recovering in some tentative fashion. He wasn't drinking any more. There was no one in the house to drink with. He was smoking less, because he had to do it outside in the cold. As the winter waned and the light began to return to the rooms of Mrs. Miller's big bungalow, Earl was showing signs of energy. On his good days, he became the house volunteer, attending to the needs of the ladies in small ways, wielding the raygun to change channels on the big set in the living room, fetching fruit-juice from the fridge, shovelling the driveway and the front sidewalk after a snowfall. If he could believe from time to time that he was doing a job at Mrs. Miller's rather than merely waiting there to die, then life at Supreme Home Care was almost bearable.

Usually it was anything but. His moods were up and down like the stock market. On the bad days he was miserable, sharptongued, louder than he needed to be, restless as a caged coyote. On such days, before getting up in the morning, he imagined the onset of his own death like a slow and gradual freeze followed by eternal silence. The only defense against such imaginings was to leap up from his bed and get moving. When he felt strong enough, he would go for a stroll in Mrs. Miller's brand new suburb.

No one seemed to know how it came to be called Vista Lake. There was no lake within miles, nor had there ever been. The neighbourhood was a bewildering set of loops, crescent after crescent of large treeless homes, many of which resembled one another to such an extent that Earl would get lost among the loops. His daily walks became part of a larger plan to be the first one ever to escape Mrs. Miller's home alive. If he wanted out, he would have to get in shape. Bewildering as they often were, the daily strolls began to take on an air of urgency. But how to make them interesting, that was the question.

One day he spied a narrow public walkway between two hedges that led downhill through the neighbourhood loops and all the way to the river. It felt like an escape route, an underground railway for old farts. On his way back up to the house, he memorized the crescent and the addresses between which lay the entrance to his newly discovered path. As the winter drew to a close, this walk down to the river became Earl's greatest respite from the death that stalked him at Mrs. Miller's. On his good days, Earl would weave his way through the crescents to his path and down to the river and gawk at joggers and dog walkers.

LUCK

Getting back up to Mrs. Miller's, however, was a challenge. Since his release from the hospital, he had lost something, that mysterious force that used to keep him up and doing. In his present condition, he had enough energy to walk downhill, roam around a bit, but then he was faced with an uphill walk of about a mile. He had to do it in segments, resting two or three times. He would sit on curbs or lean on fences and hope the residents of his new suburb didn't look askance at him. People these days seemed unusually guarded, and especially protective of their kids. Earl gradually settled on his favourite spots for hunkering down to catch his breath. He could not sit down on the public path because it was too narrow, and he'd look like some kind of nut escaped from God knows where. So he took his longest rests in two places. Rest spot number one, at the foot of the path, looked down on the river. Rest spot number two, at the head of the path, was just a curb in a cul-de-sac on a quiet crescent. Residents would park their cars nearby and sometimes nod politely at him. People on foot would notice that he was puffing, come up to him, ask if he needed assistance. He would shake his head and explain that he was just out for a stroll. They always talked to him as though he were ninety-six, not sixty-six.

On the morning after the visit from the mysterious stranger, Earl was convinced that he was ready to leave Mrs. Miller's establishment forever. He had hinted once or twice to her in that direction. He hadn't seen his old house since before the break-in. But it was still there, the jimmied back door boarded up, waiting for his return. Why not just pack his bag, walk out the door and not come back? It might be tough for a while cooking his own meals, straightening up the house, shopping without a car, but perhaps he could hire someone to take care of him. He had almost finished his daily walk, and he was sitting on the curb. He was wondering what a fair wage for the job would be, when a boy walked towards him carrying a canvas bag, a paper boy.

"Got an extra?" Earl asked. He pulled out a loonie and handed it to the boy. "I useta do that," he said. "Long time ago."

The boy gave him an old-fashioned salute and moved on up the crescent. The salute was two fingers touching the cap. Earl hadn't seen that gesture for a long time. That was how you greeted someone in his neighbourhood way back in the forties and fifties. You raised your hand to your cap. Two fingers, index and middle finger, the same two fingers

59

you used to form a gun and shoot someone at recess. You touched the cap as if to say *Good mornin to you, Sir. Fine mornin.*

No one talked like that anymore. No one gave that salute. Maybe, Earl thought, it's come back. All the rage with the young people. Or maybe, if you were a paper boy, you learned that salute from an older paper boy, who learned it from an older paper boy as though it had been passed on down the line from the first one in history to this one in Vista Lake. He glanced up at the boy and saw himself walking away.

Earl returned to Mrs. Miller's in time for a smoke with Julie. Regardless of the temperature outside, she needed her smoke breaks as much as Earl. They'd weathered the winter side by side, puffing away for a few minutes each day on the cold patio, exchanging gossip and racy jokes. Her saucy wit and his lunch-bucket humour seemed a good match.

"Earl, you just missed him again."

"The doctor?"

"No, the guy, the fella who come by yesterday. You know."

"Oh, you mean your mystery man, the bill collector."

"Yeah," said Julie. "Said he'd be back."

"Well, did you get his name this time?"

As Earl unfolded his copy of the *The Saskatoon Star-Phoenix*, Julie tried to recall the man's name, muttering variations to herself. Earl was beginning to dread discovering the man's identity. Strangers who come to your door and leave no card were usually the bearers of bad news. Cops or doctors. Would doctors do that to a man? More likely it was a cop. Earl turned his attention to the front page and looked up from his deck chair. He was thinking once more about the paper boy. Most of them these days, girls too, were using metal shopping carts, but this one had been toting a big dirty canvas bag just like the one…

"Julie, who brings the paper here?"

"You asked the right person," she said. "His name is Sammy. He's my kid."

"I'll be damned." Earl pondered this news for a moment. "At least you can remember his name, Julie. You're one for two today."

"None a yer sass, Earl."

Julie turned to peer at him from the corner of her eye. "Why do you ask?"

"I seen him on the way up from my walk. Nice lookin kid."

"Takes after his mom."

"You mean he's got trouble rememberin names too?"

Julie slapped Earl's knee.

"Say, Mrs. M. told me you might not last here. She says you were thinkin of goin back home? What's goin on, Earl?"

"Oh, nothin." Earl lowered his voice to a rasp. "I told her coupla times I couldn't afford to live here too much longer. I mean if this thing I got," Earl pointed to his head, "if this really is on the wane, I might just hightail it back to my house. Before the summer. You know what I pay per month here? Yeah? Well then, you know it's not cheap."

Julie stubbed out her cigarette on the side of the tin can and made as though to stand.

"Takes a lotta bread, that's true."

"I won a lottery once," said Earl. "Bet you didn't know that, eh. Back in '93. It wasn't no million bucks, it was one a them Forty-nine ones, eh, and that's what I been livin on."

"Wow. Lucky or what."

"Hundred thou, more or less."

"You got horseshoes, Earl."

The exact figure was one hundred and twenty thousand dollars. It was the most unexpected kind of luck Earl had ever seen, but it hadn't felt lucky. It had come a month or two after Earl's wife died. He spent a big chunk of it on high living, buying himself and his friends a lot of beer, going to the races and just plain forgetting. When he finally put a halt to his spending and got down to grieving, there was still forty-four thousand left in a term deposit and a chequing account at the Credit Union. Now there was twenty-nine thousand and a monthly pittance from Old Age Security, enough to keep him at Mrs. Miller's for one more year. Seemed a waste of good cash.

"Hell," he said, and rose from his chair on the patio. "It's not just the money."

"Shh."

"She downstairs?"

Julie nodded.

"I don't want no more a this place," Earl whispered. "It's all right for them old gals. They've run the race and they need someone to take care a them."

Julie nodded.

"Thing is," Earl said, "I did them tests not long ago, right? Any day now the docs are gonna phone me, tell me right out where I'm *at* type a deal. Any day now."

Julie had to get back in. There were women to clean, beds to change, laundry to do.

"You don't spose that fella keeps askin for me, you don't spose—"

"A doctor? Are you kiddin, Earl? No doctor in this town would make a house call if he could use a phone."

Earl had begun to phone his friends in the old neighbourhood, and through the latter part of February he had pieced together the gossip, the state of his burgled and boarded-up house, the friends who had fallen by the wayside, the state of service in the beverage room of the King Eddy. He still would not divulge his new address at Mrs. M's place, he had his reasons, but he had allowed his friends to know that he was still in the ball game, and that there were no plans for a funeral in the near future. All he needed, he had said to his friends and to himself, was the word from the doctors, and he was gone.

No word had come. He had left messages with his doctor's receptionist. "If he's too busy to come out here and see me, let him phone the results. I got my own phone here, yknow."

And then, "How long does it take to check out a coupla a drops of blood an a bottle a piss? How long does it take to have yer X-ray developed? Hell, I can get a film done same day at the christly drugstore."

And later, "You can tell me the truth, y'know. I'm not afraid a the goddam truth. You guys up there in your offices, you're not dealin with some pussy who calls for his mommy every time he gets a scraped knee. Am I dyin or am I livin, it's a real simple question."

And finally, "You don't send someone out here to talk turkey with me, someone who knows a stethoscope from a dildo, I'm comin down there to raise some shit."

One morning in early March a man showed up at Supreme Home Care. He wanted to know where he and Earl could talk privately. They went out to the patio and sat in the deck chairs.

"Someone told me you guys didn't do house calls," said Earl.

"Sometimes it's all we do," said the man.

"What's your name again?" said Earl.

The man told him his name, sounded Jewish.

"You're not a doctor?"

"No, Mr. Claney, I'm an investigator," he said. "I've been checking some old court records. Just a few questions and I'm on my way."

"You the guy keeps tryin to talk to me?"

The man nodded.

"You the one handling the investigation?"

The man seemed confused.

"The break-in. My house got burgled last month."

"I didn't know about the break-in, no," the man said. "But I'm not a cop. I'm investigating for a client."

"Yer a private eye?"

"I'm what they call a special investigator," said the man. "The city retains me to work on old cases, old files. I used to be a cop but I turned in my badge some years ago."

Claney peered at his visitor and offered him a cigarette, but the man declined. He looked about Earl's age, healthier, more energetic, stocky, built close to the ground. Big nose.

"I dig into old files," the man said. "Sometimes it's just an insurance claim or a law suit. Don't worry," he added, "I don't arrest people."

"Old cases," Earl heard himself say. His voice was sounding guarded, his chest felt tight. He wondered if Julie or Mrs. Miller could hear the conversation from inside the kitchen.

"It's my brother, ain't it," said Earl in a low voice.

"Yes."

"Jesus. That was a long time ago." Earl could hear the quiver in his own voice.

The man had taken out a tatty old notebook. He was flicking the pages for what seemed a rather long time, and at last he looked up.

"A few things about you and your brother, Mr. Claney." He paused. "If that's all right with you."

Without any warning, as though the memory of his brother's disappearance could provoke all the forces of nature, a wind passed through the backyard and swayed the trees along the fence. A weather front was upon them. It felt like the chaotic presence of his brother come back from the depths of the flooded river for a final reckoning. It felt like the last call at the King Eddy, the beginning of the end, the Day of Judgement. All these things. Earl's visitor looked up at the swaying trees with some concern, as though perhaps he shared some of Earl's ruminations.

"I've forgotten your name," Earl said.

"Shmata," the man said, handing him a card. "People have trouble with it."

Earl reached down for the tin can where dozens of his and Julie's butts were stored. He stubbed out his cigarette on the inside of the can and looked up at his visitor.

"What do you think these burglars were looking for? In your house, I mean."

"God only knows," Earl muttered, struggling to his feet. His head was swimming. He was waiting for the return of the telltale coloured lights, the sign of another seizure. He closed his eyes, swayed, clutched the side of his lawn chair, and his head cleared.

"Kids nowadays, they bust into a house, looks like nobody's home so they wreck the place. Hepped up on drugs an booze."

"Could be," said Shmata, offering his arm to Earl, who shrugged it off.

"You know somethin about it?"

"No."

Earl indicated to Shmata by flapping his hand that they go to his room at the back of the house. The man followed him. Earl closed the door, sat down on the bed, and Shmata sat down on the room's only chair.

"Do you read the papers, Mr. Claney?"

Earl glared at the man. "Now an then."

"Did you happen to hear about the double slaying in Vancouver last month?"

"Mighta seen somethin on the television. What's that got to do with my brother?"

"I hate to take you all the way back to that time," said Earl's visitor. "Most people would probably like to forget about the murder of a brother."

"Fifty-two years ago."

"Fifty-two years, yes."

Earl continued to stare at the floor. He could hear the moaning wind outside his window.

"So?" Earl said. "My brother Joey's dead and the guy done it went to jail. Bulger. You got that in your notebook?"

"Yes, Mr. Claney, but at the time there was some suspicion that others had put the killer up to it. Encouraged Bulger, they said. Nothing was proven, but the suspicion remains that Bulger was acting on behalf of his friends."

"Them bastards at the hotel, that's who they were. Them Judas bastards Joe worked with."

"Your brother told you, did he?"

"Now I didn't say that."

Earl had once more forgotten his visitor's name. He checked the card. *William Shmata, Special Investigator.*

"Do the names Bishop Montgomery or Lamont Spencer mean anything to you?"

"Say that first name again."

"Bishop Montgomery?"

"Yeah," said Earl. "Maybe I hearda that guy. He was on the bridge the day my brother got throwed off. Didn't lift a finger. I seen him at the trial. Thought the sun shone outa his arsehole. Bishop Montgomery. Holy Mother a…you mean he was one a them guys on the television? The guys that got murdered?"

The investigator nodded.

"Jesus H. Christ."

"Were you here last month?"

"I was here. I live here now. Ask anyone. Ask Julie."

The investigator was scratching his scalp and glaring down from where he sat on the chair, as though he had lost some change on Earl's floor. A restless fellow, this one.

"Mr. Claney, I read a report that you were picked up in Banff about ten years ago for disturbing the peace. What was that all about?"

"Nothin much. I got drunk. Hassled some people."

"But why? And why these particular people? Employees at a hotel, working people."

"Drunk," said Earl.

"You're on record with some complaints that your brother's case needed to be re-investigated. Remember those phonecalls you used to make? As far as I can tell, you'd never broken the law. Even your brother Joseph had more trouble with the authorities than you did. And then you get charged at the same hotel where your brother was working just before his death all those years ago. Am I supposed to think this was all a coincidence?"

"I don't remember," said Earl, which was partly true. "I hassled some people because I was pissed off. I hassled this German guy because I found out some things. He'd worked at the same place as my brother. A career bellboy for godsake. And he was an asshole. Enda story."

"What was his name?"

"Grousen, somethin like that. William fuckin Grousen. What about that Bulger bastard? You ask him who done the killings?"

"Mr. Bulger died in prison."

"Well well. There's a God in Heaven."

"Your testimony must have carried some weight, don't you think?"

"The guy was guilty as sin. Two cops seen him do it. You must know that."

The investigator had found something in his notebook. He pointed to a page and peered at Earl. "He threw your brother over the bridge after an altercation. There seems to be no doubt of that. But they never found a body, Mr. Claney, and when that happens, the man would ordinarily get charged with manslaughter."

"So?"

"Unless, of course, there is strong evidence that the offender had planned to kill his victim from the start." Shmata thumped his notebook with a knuckle. "And you provided that evidence, didn't you, Mr. Claney."

"I just told em what I knew."

"You spoke with your brother in Saskatoon just before he was killed. Was that when he told you that Bulger had planned to kill him?"

Claney shrugged. "Guess so."

"Well, Mr. Claney, you must remember testifying against Bulger. When you told the court how Bulger was gunning for your brother, he had to be restrained. You must remember that."

"Y'ask me," Earl muttered, "the guy was nuts."

"Or he was left holding the bag for Montgomery and Spencer."

"Mebbe he was. But—"

"Judas bastards, you called them?"

"Yeah, so what?"

"It must really have galled you, Mr. Claney, that these two fellows never got charged. Sounds to me like they had a pretty good lawyer."

Claney shrugged. The man named Shmata scribbled something down, rose from the bed, flipped his pad closed.

"Suppose, Mr. Claney, that one night you were to pick up the telephone. One angry night you picked it up. Would this William Grousen also end up dead?"

"Hah," said Earl, without passion. "You think that's what I done? Picked up a telephone an these two rich bastards got killed? Me? I might wanna dance a jig at their funerals but you gotta be outa your mind."

"Just wondering," the man said.

At last Shmata left the room, and Earl remained on the bed, staring at the place where the man had sat. When Mrs. Miller came to call him for supper, his room was growing dark.

DARK

Saskatoon, mid–March 2003

After his interview with Earl Claney, Shmata drove home beneath an advancing dark wall of clouds and a steady wind. Earl Claney's ghost, or at least his shadow, seemed to accompany Shmata in the car as he drove. It followed him all the way to his little townhouse and waited in the kitchen while Shmata surveyed the food in his fridge. He discovered a styrofoam container half-filled with chow mein. He sniffed it and set it down on the kitchen table. Earl Claney was right there, a disapproving presence gazing at the chow mein. Shmata couldn't help feeling a certain affection for Earl. Scrawny as an old chicken. The sort of affection one feels for someone who isn't going to be sticking around for long. The man was hiding something, but at the end of their interview, Claney had tightened up, gone vague, and that was the end of that.

Shmata went back to the fridge and located some soya sauce and a small container of cold rice, a pair of chopsticks in a drawer. He squatted on a chair and began poking around in the chow mein container, munching apathetically and wondering about his assignment from Letourneau. Who would be angry at Shmata when he found out about his interview with Earl Claney. Who still seemed to be glaring at him from across the kitchen table.

He glared back at Claney, closed his eyes, yawned, and beheld an equally displeased Mike Letourneau. Displeased? Royally pissed off. Going against Letourneau's orders was a chance he'd had to take. He'd gotten off to a slow start, just dragging his feet, and spent the rest of the week digging out and reading trial transcripts, following up reports in the file, getting an old buddy at the Service to do some phone snooping, and he'd had to get closer to the action than the Courthouse storage room.

But where exactly had it gotten him? Shmata tried to tally the scraps gleaned from his interview with Claney. Now, at least, he could confirm that Earl Claney was in no condition to have bludgeoned two men to death. Secondly, Claney had referred to the murder victims in Vancouver as *them Judas bastards*, so in Earl's eyes, they may have put Bulger up to his attack on Earl's brother on the CPR Bridge those many years ago. That was still a possibility. Earl Claney had obviously been nursing a grudge against Bishop Montgomery, though how big a grudge was anyone's guess. And Shmata now had a new lead to follow. He had the name of a man who, if he was still alive, might remember some things about Joe Claney's murder. William Grousen.

Shmata gave up on his chow mein and glanced out the kitchen window. It was getting darker, still windy, but there was still no storm. He could drive over to Letourneau's house and explain his actions, make his apologies. No warning phonecalls. Just drop in for a friendly chat and spill the beans. He arose from the kitchen table and bade good evening to the aura of Earl Claney.

Shmata was looking up at the icy road. His car was stopped at a red light at the corner of Unger and Queen. He had driven right past the turnoff to Letourneau's house.

He'd been doing that a lot lately; he had become preoccupied, almost too much so to function in his confined little world. He kept getting stuck in his thoughts or stuck in the past, stuck in his grievances. If his own friends acted this moody and self-involved, he would avoid them. A woman at his Thursday night meeting said he was probably deep into the grieving process. He'd heard this somewhere before, a theory that did not rest well with him.

Grieving, no. Just stuck. Just spinning his wheels. He would have to move on. That's what he replied any time they cornered him at the meetings: he was moving on, he was determined to get unstuck. Grieving was for people who believed that if they got in touch with *their true feelings* they would somehow be *set free*. Grieving was for people who assumed the victim stance with a shameless lack of hesitation. Surely there were other stances available.

Move on. He would have to move on. He would have to move on from a lot of things. Some broken relationships. A drinking habit that started decades ago. A case that haunted him to this day, the Walter case, his one and only serial killer. Who was dead and buried and quite possibly warming a place in hell for Bill Shmata. Then there was his ongoing discontent with the Saskatoon Police Service over his re-instatement. A whole lot to move on from, but move on he would.

Shmata looked up again at the traffic lights, and right then his light turned green. There you go. Bill Shmata rested his case.

But where, exactly, was he going with this investigation of Letourneau's? What was the basic idea here? To investigate Earl Claney to see if he had enough of a grudge to send a killer after his brother's co-workers from the summer of 1951? It sounded preposterous. A fifty-two year-old grudge acted on this year? He had looked into Claney's phone and banking records leading up to February's double murder and drawn a blank. The next move would be to check and see if William Grousen was still alive. Letourneau would approve.

Letourneau had managed to suck him into this job with rumours of a hoard of silver dollars. A cheap trick that had worked. Maybe Shmata should drop in on Letourneau and pump him for some more facts. He may well have been hiding something.

But Shmata had driven past the turnoff to Letourneau's house. On impulse he kept going south, parallel to the river, skirting the downtown, and over to Riversdale, Claney's old neighbourhood. There was still some light in the western sky. He parked in front of Earl's place, a small frame house, 1920s vintage, freshly painted, white with royal blue trim, neat as a pin. No one was on the street. Shmata got out of his car and strolled to the back of Claney's house where the break-in had occurred. The walks were slushy with melted ice and snow. He climbed the stoop to the back door, which had been boarded over, perhaps by a neighbour. He peeked into a back window, shuffled around to the front again and returned to his car.

He took a spin down the block and began to drive the streets of Earl's former neighbourhood. Old frame houses, some freshly painted in pink and robin's egg blue. The colours in this part of town reminded him of the inside of an Orthodox church. He drove out to Market Street and glanced at the King Edward Hotel. According to the woman who worked at Claney's care home, this was Claney's watering hole. It slouched on the corner like a panhandler.

Shmata drove on, heading back into the neighbourhood. One block from Claney's front door was a street that ran parallel to the river, curving as the river curved in a wide arc. It took him past the old Sanatorium, and like Earl Claney's home, there was no sign of human habitation. The walks had not even been shovelled. The word in *The Saskatoon Star-Phoenix* was that the San was slated for dismantling later in the spring. Another grand old building gone. The main structure loomed over the well-treed grounds as though it were built for more than just its own time.

Shmata drove past the waterworks and the tennis club, the canoe club, all venerable establishments on the lunch bucket side of town. There was something appealing about an old working-class neighbourhood, a kind of hard knocks gentility that you didn't find on the east side. He knew this area from his days in the patrol car. More and more, the old houses around here were being bought up by absentee landlords and rented out to hard scrabble tenants who paid the rent with welfare cheques and spent the rest on booze and other recreational delights. A year or more ago, according to the police report, there had been a drug raid only a few doors down from where Earl Claney had lived. But on the break-in to Earl's house, it had been brief and inconclusive, without the usual list of stolen goods. The investigating officers had concluded that there was some possibility the break-in had been done by juveniles looking for items to pawn.

Shmata had lost his resolve to have a talk with Letourneau. Perhaps tomorrow he could talk with the woman who had worked up the file for him. The researcher, Bertha Eeling. And then talk with Letourneau. *Mike*, he would say, *I've done a no-no*. He checked himself, started up the car again. No, you never give Letourneau an out-and-out apology or he'll jump on you. *Mike*, he would begin, *about that conversation we had last week*.

He drove home in the dark and when he got inside the townhouse, he was greeted once more by the ghostly aura of Earl Claney.

SHORTY REMEMBERS

Saskatoon, early March 2003

Earl was slumped on his bed in the faded light. He was digging around in the summer of 1951. In a life full of discarded memories, there were still a few that murmured over and over again like an irritating song. No joy in this particular memory: an early morning in August, a garage in the laneway. Shale dust and a smell of decay. Earl was drifting back now, closer and closer to Joey.

"It's time for your supper, Earl. Let's go."

"Who says there's no such thing as ghosts?"

"What's that?" blared Mrs. Miller.

"Nothin. Never mind. I ain't hungry."

That time when Joey came back, it was about six in the morning. Warm day. Dry weather. Joe just barely a man, and Earl barely a teenager. To feel that godawful time coming back to him, by the Jesus, that was weird. Slowly Earl stood up from the bed, shook his head. The memory stood up as well, followed Earl across the room like a dog begging to go for a walk. He fumbled in his dresser drawer beneath a T-shirt and pulled out a faded green card. He squinted at the object, an old scorecard with some writing on it. He should give it to Julie and she could give it to her son, Sammy. He crumpled the card and stared out the window.

He must be seriously depressed. Why else would he get all hung up about something that happened so long ago? It was the goddam investigator who was responsible for this weird turn of affairs. William Shmata. Earl had been doing just fine before that asshole darkened his doorway. He'd been almost ready to move back home again.

"Joey Claney, are you listenin?"

Silence.

"Who are you talkin to, Earl?"

It was Julie Belanger this time.

"I don't want no supper. I'll eat later."

"Well, Earl, can I at least turn on the light?"

"No. Leave me be."

Earl began to shake. "I was talkin to my brother, the Great Houdini." He was shaking, couldn't stop.

"Looks to me like you're havin an episode, Earl," Julie said. "You sure I can't get you somethin?"

Fear was in the room. You could smell it, you could smell the fear seeping into you. Sulphur. Smelled like a goddam pulp mill. The coloured lights were coming round the bend. They danced on the bedspread and around the one window in his room and swarmed in by the dresser. Orange lights, green lights, all sorts of Christmas tree colours, downtown neon lights. They glittered and sparked on the shoulders of Julie Belanger. Heaving up and down, waves of craven fear like ocean swells sent the lights pulsing to the rhythm of his heart.

"Earl, you just sit still and don't move, okay? I'll be right back."

The very moment Julie's footsteps receded, Earl was walking away, carrying his suitcase home, no, carrying his sack. He was Shorty now, not Earl. His hands began to fidget, then his legs. He was afraid. Because he had to meet up with Mister Trouble himself, and he had a route to complete and the bag, the big canvas bag, it was tugging on his shoulder. The muscles between his neck and his left shoulder hurt so bad that he might just have to sit down.

He lugged the bag into the lane. Three houses down: therefore, three garages down. On the right. And there he was, Mr. Trouble. As though nothing in all the world was amiss. Mister Big Talk, King of the Block, Joseph Claney, smiling his bitter smile.

He came trudging up to Earl, lugging a golf bag with no clubs. He had a funny way of walking with his feet turned out instead of straight. Joey set down the golf bag with a heavy clank and checked his watch. Shifty-eyed and slouching like a much older man. He seemed to be listening for something. Earl tried to speak. He opened his mouth. The words were all lined up: *Mornin, Joey. Been a long time.* But the words would not come out. Why wouldn't the words come out? Why were his hands fidgeting? Why were his feet fidgeting? *Mornin, Joe. It's been a long...it's been a real long...*

The sun was already up and it made Joey squint. If you did not know him, you would think he was grinning. Earl walked up to him, hauling his twenty-five-pound sack of newspapers. His big brother tried to sound casual.

"Shorty."

"Joe."

"Long time no see."

Joe shouldered the golf bag (he'd probably stolen it) and looked around one last time. With a wag of his head, he motioned Shorty to follow him inside the old shed. The side door was stuck and he had to push with some force.

"How come you didn't stay with us last night?"

"Had some things needed doing."

"What's in the golf bag?"

"Oh, you'll see, little brother."

They each lugged their bags up to the entrance of the shed, and at that moment they looked like brothers: a burly young man of twenty who spoke from an old man's slouch, and a thirteen year-old with a skinny version of the same slouch and similarly pomaded black hair. Here they were in an alley while most of Saskatoon was still in bed.

Joe checked up and down the lane one more time but there was no one around.

"So, what's goin on? Whadja phone me for?"

"What if I told you I got somethin special in this golf bag, Shorty?"

"Yeah?"

He smiled down at his brother. "Don't just say *yeah*. This is serious stuff, Shorty. This is big time. This is a matter of life an death, okay?"

"Yeah?"

"Jesus, Mary and Joseph."

They entered the sagging shed. Joe dropped his golf bag on the gravel floor, and the dust puffed up around it.

"Shorty, remember when I used to disappear?"

This sounded like more of his older brother's bullshit. This was going to be a long day.

"Hey? Member that? Not so long ago. Six years ago, seven years?"

Earl unshouldered his sack of newspapers.

"You was always a bugger for disappearin," he said.

It was true, his big brother had been a sort of amateur magician, and disappearing was what he did best. They played a game at the old San at night where Joe hid close by and the little kids had to find him. He always seemed to stump them.

74

Joe closed the side door and turned back to his brother. He was fumbling around for his lighter.

"Joey, come on, I gotta get goin."

"Shorty," he said suddenly, "just suppose I disappeared again. I mean, just suppose I disappeared for a long time."

Earl gave his older brother a cautious look.

"I mean, it could be forever, Shorty, or it could be for like a few years."

"Yeah?"

"Yeah yeah yeah. Don't say that! You make me a nervous wreck."

Shorty prodded the golf bag with his shoe and let out a lungful of air. "Joey, what in the goddam hell is on your mind?"

"Shh!"

"You always do this."

"Okay, okay."

Hunched over in the gloom of the shed, Joe lit up a smoke, opened the side door, spat in the dirt, and listened for something. The only sounds were birds and a light wind rattling through the leaves.

"Shorty, I might just have some trouble in here too."

"Is that why you didn't come home? We haven't seen you in months an you finally come to town from wherever—"

"Shorty, don't sweat the nickle dime stuff. I been workin in Banff. Now pay attention here. I phoned you, didn't I? Well, I done it for a reason, so shut your face."

Joe returned to the golf bag. "There's some money in here, Shorty. A lot a money. We could buy a car with this. We could wait till you're sixteen. Then we could buy you a big jeezly brand new car, I mean absolutely nothin owing. We could take a trip down to the States. Anywhere. But it's like…it's like Robin Hood money, Shorty."

Shorty could only gawk at his brother.

"You know, rob from the rich? Well, it's mine now."

Shorty nodded.

"Would you like to have some of this money, Shorty? Wouldn't that be swell?"

Shorty frowned at his sack of fifty Saturday papers.

"Yer mouth's open, Shorty. Would you like half a this money? Hey?"

Joe hunkered down on some old shiplap. He was whispering again.

"Shorty, here's what we do. We switch loads. I throw some rocks and heavy stuff in here and take a few of your papers an I stuff em in this here golf bag, eh? And you take this. I mean all of it. You haul it off in your paper sack."

"What about my rags?" said Shorty. "They don't get delivered, I'm out of a job."

His brother didn't answer him. He drew out a cigar box, rattling with coins, from the golf bag. He laid it down and pulled out a leather pouch. It was almost as big as a loaf of bread. Then a canvas bag about the same size, and another one. He kept pulling bags out until six more canvas sacks were lying in the dust. Then a smaller one, a bulging Seagram's bag made of soft purple cloth, and another one. He opened one of the canvas bags and took out a large roll of coins.

"These are from a bank or somethin," Joe said. "Oh, wait."

He reached down into the bottom of the golf bag and pulled out a big wool sock. From the sock he extracted a fat roll of bills and a handful of silver coins.

"Looka that, eh? Sawbucks an twenties in there."

"Where'd you—"

"Never mind," Joe whispered. "I'll tell ya later. And you can do your rags later this mornin. We leave em right here, see? Now look, there's a lotta money in here. I tried to count it on the train, eh? In the can? But guys kept knockin on the door so I had to quit. *There was too jeezly much to count it all!* Now don't say nothin, Shorty, an we'll both have a nice big pile of pin money. I mean *a lot* of pin money. Trust me, okay? Say you'll trust me."

Earl took a deep breath. He would not look his brother in the eye. He refocussed his gaze on the darkest corner of the garage.

Joe grabbed Shorty's newspaper sack and emptied it on the floor. One by one he placed the money bags into the great dusty sack. He laid some papers on top of the load, picked the sack up and swung it over his burly right shoulder. "Can you carry this now, Shorty?" he said.

"Of course I can carry it."

"Can you carry this all the way home? I know a spot where you could stash it."

"I don't want no trouble."

"Shorty, call me Houdini."

Shorty just glared at his brother. Everything his mother had said about Joey was coming true. A trouble maker, guy with the big plans and the shady deals, a talker.

Joey placed a brick and several big stones inside the golf bag, raised it up so that they would fall to the bottom, then he scrounged some spikes and a few handfuls of large nails from an old paint can and dumped them in too. At last he stuffed newspapers into the top of his golf bag and kept peering up at his younger brother.

"For old times sake," said Joe.

Shorty was not going to get into this. Not today, not any day. He wouldn't even look at his brother.

"Comeon, for old times sake. Houdini, Shorty. Don't tell me you don't remember."

Finally Shorty glared right at him. "Know what everybody called you when I was a kid? They called you Joe Claney the big talker."

"Well fuck you too."

"I'm not your little messenger no more. It's not that way, I got things to do."

"Shorty, don't you see? I might not come back here for a long time. Some guys are lookin for me and they're not very nice, okay? They're a bunch of high life blueblood cheats and bastards. So if I don't never come back you can have it all. The whole shootin match."

Joey was waiting. He had never sounded more sincere.

"Shorty, for chrissakes, these guys. They catch me with this money, you know what they'll do?"

He drew a finger across his neck.

"Shorty, you can give the money away. You can give it to Mum an Sadie, you can give it to the orphanage down the street. Will you please do this for me?"

Shorty looked away and nodded.

"You're a swell brother, Shorty. Thank you. You're the best brother I ever coulda had an that's no crap. By God, you're the new king a the block, Shorty. King a the block."

Joey stood up slowly, just enough to see the street through the dusty windows of the shed. He butted out his smoke on the window ledge. They both listened, but still the only sounds were nesting birds and the morning breeze moving through the elms. He crouched down again on his knees, licking what appeared to be blood from his lower lip. He pulled out a piece of paper from his pants pocket and showed it to Shorty.

"What's this?"

"It's a present," said Joey.

"It's a scorecard," said Shorty. "It doesn't even have no golf scores."

"See those names?" Joe said.

"Yeah."

"Well?"

"I can't read their writing."

"This one's Bing Crosby. Looka that one, eh? That one's easy to read. *It says Good luck Bob Hope.*"

Earl stared at the scorecard. He shook his head. "You seen these guys up at Banff?"

"Yeah, I met them. I'll tellya about it some day. You know, Shorty, you shouldn't give this money away. You should keep it for yourself. You deserve it."

"Yeah?"

"I owe you, Shorty. I don't owe nothin to nobody around here, but I owe you."

Earl looked away once more. He'd heard this all before.

Joe said, "Remember how I used to disappear?"

"Yeah?"

"Yeah, yeah, yeah! Do you *remember*, Shorty?"

"Behind the old San."

"Right! And do you remember where?"

"By them trees."

"Did you kids ever figure out where I disappeared to?"

"I guess maybe you just clum up one a them bushy trees, one a them Christmas trees."

"Nope. I went down, not up."

"Down?"

"Remember a bunch of big old metal contraptions? On the grass like? They looked like...they looked like big over-size stovepipes an tin roofs an stuff?"

"You mean them air vents?"

"That's it, you're right, Shorty. They must a been air vents. Well, they aren't nailed down to nothin. They're not that heavy. You just lift em up an climb inside an down you go."

"I always thought them things was attached."

"Nosirree, some a them go right down into the storage place, the root cellar for the kitchen."

"A cellar?"

"For potatoes an stuff. There's ladders that go right straight down. You can hide anything. There's a room off to the side. No one uses that room. You could put your newspaper bag in there an maybe put some boards over top. There used to be some boards down there. Or wait, you could dig a hole. It's a dirt floor, eh? But you'd need a flashlight."

"People would see me goin over there."

"Not if you took this home, come back and did your rags, and waited till night time."

"Why don't *you* do this? Joey?"

Joe put his finger to his lips. A car was coming down the lane. He seized the newly stuffed golf bag by the straps and slowly rose to his feet. The car went past their hiding place and headed towards the river.

"Shorty, those guys I told you about. There's two a them. They drove all the way from Banff. Even found out that we live around here. Probably still parked in front of Turner's house. I slept with the Turner boys last night and these two seen me go inside. They've been there all night long and they're just waitin. I'm gonna walk right past them and stroll down Unger Drive to the bridge, okay? In fact, I might just go all the way down to the CPR bridge. Last night before I phoned you I got this idea, see? I was gonna hide all this money myself, but these guys, they'd follow me and they'd never leave go, eh? They'd always be after me. But I got this idea. Anyways, I can take care a them."

Joe Claney's hand was on the door. "We shoulda got together more often, Shorty. It's been a while, hey?"

"Can I go now?"

"Wait till I'm gone. Wait right here. They're in a big black Dodge. Let em see me go, then you walk up the lane with your newspaper bag like you was doin the rest of your route. And then you're on your own. It's up to you, Shorty."

"Where'll you go?"

"Nowheres. I'll just do this one little thing. With the CPR bridge, see? I'll fake em out. I'll do another Houdini if I have to. I'm still the Great Houdini, Shorty. Nothin changes, hey?"

He smiled his old bitter smile, stood by the door of the shed, and shouldered the golf bag.

"Bye, little brother."

"Seeya."

"Seeya, Houdini."

Joe waited by the garage door for Shorty to say it, but Earl, who was not quite so short any more, outwaited him.

The day after Joseph Claney was thrown off the bridge, Shorty came down with a fever. He moaned loud enough at night to wake his sister. His mother came in with a washrag and a basin. She dipped the rag in cool water and held it to his forehead. Later in the night he moaned and rolled about in his small bed, twisting around on the damp sheets. All the next day he slept and at last his fever broke. But still his body ached and he was too weak to get out of bed except to go to the bathroom. In spite of all the sleep he'd had, he slept right through the second night.

He dreamt about Joey. They were riding hard. They were either on horses or just pretending to be. They were being chased by some bad people, they had to get away. And then Joe Claney was running across the field by the T.B. San, around the corner of the main building, under the Christmas trees, flying past the trees, smiling like a bitter clown. *Comeon, Shorty!* he cried. *This way, down here. Everything's hunky dory! You'll be the new king a the block!*

And then Joe Claney vanished.

Wait! cried Shorty. *Wait for me!*

He knew what to do. He ran right over to the air vents.

But they were gone. The Christmas trees were gone. The grass was gone. The old San was gone.

Joe? he cried. *Joe! Wait for me! Joe!*

Finally Shorty yelled it out so loud that his sister Sadie began to call their mother. He yelled it again and again, *Wait for me*, his eyes open now and burning with strange light, even as his mother came horrified into the room: *"Houdini! Houdini! You're the Great Houdini!"*

"I've been called worse, believe you me."

Earl was slumped on his bed. A small woman was standing there. It was Julie Belanger.

"How long have I been sittin here?" he asked.

"Since supper time. You okay?"

"Yeah. Did I say anything?"

"Hah."

"What'd I say?"

"Not much. First you call me Joe, then you say you're the new king of the block. Houdini. Jesus, Earl, you had yourself one great time."

The aura of fear was gone from the room. Maybe he would have a bite to eat now.

"When Mrs. M. called me to fetch you for supper, first I thought you was ticked off at somethin," said Julie. "But the second I seen your hands shake like that, well, I knew."

She pointed to his left hand. "What's that you've got?"

Earl looked down at his hand. He was holding a crumpled piece of paper.

"A scorecard," he said. "Only thing my brother Joey ever give me that had no strings attached. See?"

"What's the writing say? Autographs?"

"Yup. Bob Hope an Bing Crosby."

"You're kiddin."

"I gotta get outa here, Julie."

"Yeah, don't we all. Here, big fella. Lean on me."

BERTHA'S FILE

Saskatoon, mid–March 2003

Shmata sought out Bertha Eeling in her small glassed-in office in the basement file-storage unit of the police building. She was underneath her desk, fiddling with a phone jack.

"Oh, hello," she sang out, and her face popped up.

"I am—"

"William Shmata. I know."

Shmata sat down in the only chair that was not stacked high with books and files.

Bertha said, "I recognize your face from, let me see, ah yes, this photograph."

She plucked an eight by ten black and white from a pile of pictures perched atop her printer and handed it to Shmata. He was dressed in a sports jacket and tie, standing between two large men, the only one not smiling. The Walter case. He couldn't seem to escape it. The large grinning man on the left was a key witness named Waller. The large grinning man on the right was Mike Letourneau. It was the late spring or early summer of 2001. By then he'd been off the force, but they'd brought him in the back door as a special investigator. The three of them were being honoured by the City of Saskatoon. Bravery or diligence, and he was feeling—you could tell from the photo—a sense of total exhaustion.

Bertha was smiling brightly. "What can I do for you today, Mr. Shmata?"

In a room surrounded by so much barrenness, a room with so little convenient shelving, with such a low budget look about it, the Bertha Eeling smile looked like an oasis of misplaced optimism.

"I'm hoping that you might have something that our friend Letourneau doesn't have."

The smile persisted. "And that would be?"

Shmata shrugged. "Some of your background material? Pictures? Anything at all on a murder investigation in 1951—"

"Aha," said Bertha. "That would be my very own Bulger/Claney file."

She stood and surveyed her small domain, then looked out the glass enclosure into the dusky rows of stacks in the storage room, then back to the chair next to Shmata's. She had perfect posture. Bertha pointed at a chair on the other side of her desk.

"Right there. It only goes to 1999. In a week or so I'm going to finish it. Oops. Don't tell a soul?"

Shmata nodded. He lifted a file from the chair to his right.

"Next one down, I believe."

Shmata could tell by the heft of the file that the information went beyond the one Letourneau had given him.

"I've been entering dozens of these files on the computer," Bertha said. "The juicy ones."

"So I hear. May I call you Bertha?"

"If I can call you Bill."

"You may indeed. Does Mike Letourneau know you have all this stuff on Joseph Claney?"

"He does," she said, "but he's never once asked to see it all. He knows what he knows. He's letting me finish the job on the Q.T. It shouldn't get out that I'm at work on an active file."

Shmata flicked through the first few pages. Her report was accompanied by a great many handwritten notes. Shmata did a brief comparison. The hotel where all the principal parties had worked in the summer of 1951 was the Hochelaga, which was just north of the Banff townsite. Check. Several of the witnesses called to testify had been bellboys. Check. Joseph Claney had been hired as a dishwasher. Check. The late Cletis Bulger, who had served time for the murder of Joseph Claney, had served some earlier time in jail, just after the war, for a rape. Check.

Where Bertha's notes diverged from the file Letourneau had passed to him, were in the small details. For example, Bulger had served during the last two years of World War II in the Canadian Navy doing tours of duty in the North Atlantic. Pinned to Bertha's file was a small snapshot of Bulger in uniform, grinning nervously for the camera. He seemed shy.

"How did you get this stuff?"

"Oh, we librarians," said Bertha.

She was peering at him bemusedly over the rims of her glasses. At most, she would be just into her fifties. Her hair was braided into a black and silver rope, thick and hemplike, and it fell over her shoulder like an afterthought, a fashion statement that seemed to disapprove of fashion.

"I just did some digging around. I got the military records from Ottawa," she said. "I quite enjoy the digging. It's fun."

Shmata flipped past the pages on Bulger until he came to Bertha's information on Joseph Claney. A stretch in a juvenile detention home for theft. Suspended sentence for attempting to drug a racehorse. A brawl outside a hotel.

"And here's an item on Joe Claney's brother Earl winning the Lotto."

"One hundred and twenty thousand dollars."

"And Letourneau hasn't read these notes?"

Bertha shrugged. "No."

The Letourneau of old would most certainly have asked for Bertha's notes. The Letourneau of old would also have ridden herd on this fax request before he dumped it off on Shmata. The Letourneau of old didn't used to repeat the phrase, *I got it covered* quite so often, like a nervous tic.

Bertha rose above the rubble on her desk.

"I'm hungry," she said. "Want to join me for lunch?"

They brought the file along and drove in Bertha's car through the downtown, parked on Twentieth Street next to a café of Bertha's choosing. Joe's Lunch was as old as Saskatoon itself. Shmata followed his stomach to the closest heart attack on a plate, a burger and fries as generous as they were greasy. Bertha ordered a large bowl of vegetable soup. Shmata excused himself and read one last note, a summary of Bulger's life in prison. He might have gotten off with less than ten years, but he killed another man in prison and attempted to burn the body in the prison incinerator. *Oh, Bertha Eeling*, Shmata said to himself. He looked up at her and caught a look of appraisal directed at him.

"Bertha, you said it was fun? Digging around and fleshing out these files is fun?"

Bertha redirected her gaze to his side of their little table, just as his evil burger arrived.

84

"Yes," she said. "This could turn into a book. Just imagine, being paid by someone to research your very own book. I was born to go over musty files and discarded photos and rescue them from the garbage bin. Sometimes I can almost hear the people in the photographs crying out for someone to tell their story."

"There's no mention of Bulger's death here."

"There will be," she said. "Next week. That's become my motto of late."

"Hmm. My guess is that either your mother or your father was a librarian of some kind."

"Not so," she said, and her voice softened. "They died in a car accident when I was just a baby. My grandad raised me. Henry Eeling, rest his soul. He loved old things," she went on. "Old books, old buildings. He and Granny were from England, and then Ontario for a while, and when they realized they'd come all the way out here to an outpost that had, well, not much sense of history, I think it must have driven them half mad. Nothing old to remind them of a past. My grandmother was obsessive about it. Apparently."

"Apparently?"

"Well, I never knew her either. She died of tuberculosis when she was still middle-aged. It was a bit before my parents' accident."

"That grandfather of yours must have been some fellow."

"Grandad was left without his wife and his only offspring, and there I was, this toddler. So he raised me. Him and a small army of nannies and neighbours. But he loved history and he loved old things."

"A Brit who finds himself in a place with no past."

"Well, he wouldn't quite admit that. He was determined to find and preserve one. He helped to start up the Heritage Society. He read any history he could get his hands on, especially anything about right here. And after he retired, he got involved in all sorts of local history projects. Natural history too. And here I am, true to the Eeling cause, a refugee from the Local History room of the Public Library. I mean, the first thing I ever sent to a public archive was my grandmother's journals. Five full volumes in little crabbed handwriting, almost illegible, except to her granddaughter. I had to type them all up on a *typewriter*, I'll have you know."

A typewriter.

"My granny must have been quite a woman," she said. "Devout in the cause of history. And wonderfully pedantic, like my grandad. Must say, I miss him."

"What did your grandfather do for a living?"

"Well, he was a teacher for a while, then a school inspector, then he ran for the Ledge. Liberal once, CCF once, defeated both times. When my grandmother passed away he tried to continue her journals for a while. She specialized in little historical discoveries, or cultural things. She was president of the Dickens Society, so whenever they had a literary event or put on a play, she would chronicle this in her diaries. When grandad became the family chronicler, he took things rapidly downhill into his own areas of expertise. Gardening, weather, walkabouts."

They talked until well past one o'clock. She was the first to notice the time. She leapt to her feet.

"Bertha, may I keep your notes and copy them?"

"If you'll do me a favour and submit to one of my interviews some day soon?"

"One of your interviews?" he said.

"For the *Annals*, of course. You must have some stories."

He recalled the photograph of himself that she had plucked from the files. "Oh, yes," he said, with no enthusiasm at all. "I've got stories."

She made him promise to guard her notes with his life, and she darted out the door. Shmata remained at the table until he had finished reading the notes in the Claney section. Bertha had provided some new names to check on—and the transportation company and a recent work number of one Wilhelm Grussen of Banff, Alberta.

William Grousen indeed. He was alive.

Shmata might have to go there, and if the city sprang for expenses, perhaps he could even stay at the Hochelaga. He'd have to square things with Letourneau, of course, make a convincing argument. Banff. Springtime in the Rockies. They'd fly him to Calgary and he could rent a car at the airport. He wondered whether he'd be able to find an AA meeting in Banff. Or a coin store.

Shmata leapt to his feet. Bertha's brisk spirit had taken him over. There were some questions that needed answering. Some easy, non-invasive ones for Earl Claney, and perhaps some tougher ones for his good friend Staff Sergeant Letourneau.

Claney first. No warning phone call. The advantage of surprise. Shmata walked, almost ran, to retrieve his car at the police building and drove out to Mrs. Miller's establishment in the Vista Lake suburbs. When he got there the March sun was doing its work in Mrs. Miller's front yard, and beige patches of dormant grass could be seen all over her lawn. It wasn't safe to proclaim to his heart that spring was here. A dangerous business, spring. You can't get caught hoping it's here, believing it's here. Good way to induce a blizzard.

He knocked on the front door, waited for a few moments, then rang the buzzer. The woman named Julie came to the door.

"You come a day too late, eh?" she said.

Her face was expressionless. Perhaps death was a frequent visitor to her place of work. Perhaps she'd had this conversation many times before.

"Mr. Claney, then, he's…"

"No, he jus took off. I tried to phone him at his house like, but the phone's cancelled. My kid, he went over there on his bike. No one home. One a the doors, eh, it's all boarded up. I start to wonder if Earl's in some kinda trouble? Hey, I think you guys better have a look."

"Gone?" said Letourneau.

He was crouched over a cup of coffee and a danish at City Perks near Shmata's townhouse. He seemed too big for the table, too big for the danish. Shmata had scarcely ever had coffee with Letourneau outside the Police Service building. In their days together on the force, they had both preferred pubs for shop talk after hours. Today Letourneau looked drugged. Anti-depressants, perhaps? Sleeping pills?

"How do you know, Shmata?"

This was probably not the best time to confess his sins to Letourneau. It was a good time to say very little and hand over the trial transcripts. They were sitting in a cardboard box at Shmata's feet.

"A woman who works at his care home."

"Jesus H. Christ, fled from a care home? Our man Claney is in hiding? I toldja he might be worth talkin to. Shmata, me boy, we're not havin a great week."

Shmata filled Letourneau in on his digging around, a heavily censored version.

"Just what am I doing here, Mike? Isn't it time I did some real investigation?"

Shmata made his bid to fly out to Banff and stay at the Hochelaga. Letourneau was browsing Bertha's *Bulger/Claney* file and yawning fitfully. "And Bolger tries to burn the other con's body, eh? Jeez."

"Letourneau, are you listening?"

"Look, Shmata, I just wired the guys in Vancouver that we'd come up with squat and we were still lookin. I gotta send them something real quick besides a weather report from Saskatoon. Why do you wanna go to the Hochelaga?"

Shmata produced his cardboard box with the copies of the court transcripts he had gathered.

"I don't want to go, Mike. But from what I can gather, that's where it all started. There's some people in Banff who were connected to this thing." *Some people* sounded better than one oldtimer. "And besides, there's bound to be some stuff in the hotel archives."

Letourneau looked up from his empty plate. In a matter of seconds, the danish had somehow vanished. His eyebrows massed like stormclouds, and Letourneau was all attention.

"What you've gathered? What are we talkin about?"

Shmata pushed the cardboard box of transcripts across the table and Letourneau put them down on his lap.

"There are people from the Hochelaga who might still remember something. Oldtimers in Banff. One of them is a trial witness by the name of Grussen. And there's no way I can handle all this by phone."

There was a certain amount of truth to this. Shmata had never had much luck doing sensitive interviews over the phone. He always liked to look at the people he interrogated, watch their body language.

"Grussen," said Letourneau.

"You've read Bertha's work on the file. Doesn't that name ring a bell?"

Staff Sergeant Letourneau had done no such thing, but where was the harm of rubbing it in?

"Should it?"

"Apparently this man was close to Bishop Montgomery during the summer of 1951. He shows up twice in the report and once in the trial transcripts. He's still alive and kicking."

Letourneau sighed mightily. He pulled out a pack of cigarettes, realized that it was 2003 and that he was not in a bar, put the cigarettes away. Yawned. He was wearing a new sports jacket, apparently fresh off the rack. Ordinarily Letourneau's taste in what he wore to work was resolutely funereal. His jackets ranged from light to dark grey. But this one was a nice light brown herringbone, and the tie was a bright red and blue silk.

"Sometimes," Letourneau was saying, "as you know, Shmata, a case gets fucked up from day one. You also know that this case was handled by a dickhead named Salter. Philip fucking Salter."

Shmata nodded.

"Philip Salter and another cop, who is also gone to cop heaven. Anyway. Some of this is not in Bertha's file. I'm not sure I want her to know about it, okay? I got most a this shit from Frenchy Demain, if you can believe it. Philip Salter was just a flatfoot back then, and he answered an early morning call. A disturbance. He and the other cop take a car down to the CPR bridge, and they climb up the stairs to the pedestrian walkway. You know, on the trestle? That bridge hasn't changed in decades."

Shmata nodded again.

"They find two guys fightin over a golf bag. An old, you know, leather golf bag. Salter goes forward to break the thing up, eh? And there's this other guy, Bishop Montgomery, he's pointing his finger at the smaller guy. There's your man, he says. Salter goes forward to break the fight up and…"

Letourneau is trying to call it up but Shmata can see that the effort is almost too much. Maybe Letourneau was right. Maybe he did have the stupids this month.

"I dunno," he says. "Things happened, I'm probably skippin some stuff. But Phil fuckin Salter, he gets this idea, he says to his partner on the bridge, let em duke it out for a while. And they did, like it was the goddam NHL. Imagine that. What was Salter thinkin? He's dead now or I'd ask him. Maybe he was afraid of heights, I mean that walkway is high, right? And before they can call a stop to this fuckin charade, the smaller guy—"

"That would be Joseph Claney?"

"Yeah, Joseph Claney, he picked up this golf bag full of money and threw it over the side. Splash. And our friend Bishop Montgomery, he gets pissed off, Bolger sees red and…"

Letourneau flapped his arms like a huge pelican.

"Bolger? Don't you mean Bulger?"

"Whatever," said Letourneau. "Oh, here's a copy of the fax I got from the boys in Vancouver. Forgot to include it in the file."

Shmata took the fax. "Is there anything *else* you forgot to give me?"

Letourneau frowned, closed his eyes, yawned.

"Mike, are you okay? Is everything—"

"What the fuck does that mean?"

About a dozen pairs of raised eyebrows turned in the direction of Shmata and Letourneau's table.

"I withdraw the question."

Letourneau glowered for a moment, took a deep breath and yawned again. "Where was I? Oh, yeah. People kept askin, was Joseph Claney dead when he hit the water? Did he drown soon after he hit the water? Did he drown later, etcetera etcetera. Did he ever drown?"

"Right, they never found the body."

"They never found the body. Bolger dumped him over the rail and he hit the river in the same spot the golf bag hit. But there'd been this…this—"

"Big rainstorm the night before," said Shmata. "I know. And the body got swept away."

Letourneau exhaled mightily. The act of telling this tale was clearly weighing on him. Or maybe life itself was weighing on him. When he spoke again, he sounded perplexed. "I mean more than fifty years ago, Shmata, fifty years. And now two guys show up dead. Can you beat that?"

"How can you be so sure it's Earl Claney? There's no chance Bulger hired someone before he died in the pen? Or someone else entirely?"

"If I was runnin this investigation, Shmata, for the boys out in Vancouver, I would say Earl Claney is our main focus. I'm not sayin he did it, I'm just sayin…"

Letourneau threw up his hands.

"By the way, when did Bulger die? Bertha hasn't gotten that far yet."

Letourneau shrugged. "Guy on the phone, he said a few years back…I think."

"Will you check—"

"I got it covered." Letourneau smiled. "Ain't that Bertha somethin?"

"Well," said Shmata, "I really think I should go to Banff. Talk with some people there. Talk to the oldtimers. Get some background on the Hochelaga. Did you know that Claney—Earl Claney, that is— got arrested for drunk and disorderly conduct because he was hassling some employees of the Hochelaga—decades after his brother was murdered?"

"Bertha told me."

"Okay, and did you know that one of these employees was a bellman named Grussen?"

Letourneau was staring off into the distance, nodding and smiling.

"We could nail this guy and send him all giftwrapped out to Steel in Vancouver. Case closed."

"Steel."

"Same asshole. He's the one who sent the fax from Vancouver asking for all this fuckin info. I'm ninety-nine percent positive."

"Martin Steel from the Walter case? The guy who lost the evidence tape?"

"Yeah," said Letourneau. "So? What are you lookin at?"

"Martin Steel. Is that why you've got me running around? You wouldn't have a little axe to grind, would you, Mike? A little revenge going on here maybe?"

"Are you calling my objectivity into doubt, William?"

"Damn rights."

"Try to imagine the headlines, Bill. Vancouver Case Solved by Saskatoon Police Service."

"Okay okay. But I have to go to Banff, Mike."

Letourneau held up his traffic stopping hand. "Maybe, Shmata. Maybe I can get you expenses."

Shmata sighed and tried not to smile. He changed the subject. "You really think it's Earl Claney?"

"I didn't say that. You're like the goddam chief, you're always puttin words in my mouth. But goddam it, Shmata, look at the facts. This guy knows somethin."

"Mike, look—"

"He knows that someone is bound to ask him some questions. He's taken off and we need to run him down. And don't talk to me about fuckin lack of objectivity, Special Investigator Shmata. I've seen you go weird about a case now an then."

Shmata said, "Don't you get the feeling this sort of a conversation should take place in the bar?"

Letourneau chuckled. "Hear hear."

I AM WILLIAM SHMATA

Saskatoon, mid-March 2003

"Say something."

"I am William Shmata, William Shmata, William Shmata."

"Good. Mr. Shmata, how long were you a regular member of the Saskatoon Police Service?"

"From 1965 to 1997. Thirty-two years."

"Your name, Shmata. Is that a Yiddish word?"

"A shmata, I think, is just an old rag. In my case it's Ukrainian—although there's some speculation that we might have been Jewish on my father's side and just didn't know it. I mean if we were, my dad would've been the last one to tell us."

"So as far as you know, your ancestors are Ukrainian."

"Yes. Mostly from Galicia."

"Do you speak any Ukrainian yourself?"

"No, not really. A few phrases. It pretty much stopped with my parents when they came to Alberta."

"Tell me about your parents."

"You sure you want to hear this stuff? I thought this was a cop reminiscence."

"It is indeed, Mr. Shmata, but I like to get some background on my subjects before they get to their stories. So, if you don't mind, your parents?"

"Dad was the barber in Vegreville, but that was the only ordinary thing about him. My mother was an old fashioned Ukrainian mom. We were closer to her than we were to my dad. Before I was born he was a revolutionary. Everything he did back in the thirties and forties was for the Cause. Sometimes the Cause was the workers. He worked in the mines down in the south of this province for a year, and later for the CPR. Big union man. Sometimes the cause was something else, like Ukrainian nationalism. Oh, and before that, the cause was...actually...communism. He went from job to job, always on the run. He was arrested more than once. A regular little rabble rouser."

"His name?"

"Dmitro Shmata. He started to lose his idealism when he found out how badly Stalin had treated the Ukrainians. He saw action in World War II, and that put an end to his idealism. He married my mother and opened the barber shop in Vegreville. For the rest of his life he walked around with a lot of bitterness against…well…"

"Against whom?"

"Well, the Anglos for one."

"Of course."

"He might have made an exception for your grandfather."

"Ha! Do you think so?"

"Who knows? But my mother was his opposite. It was best, she said, to become good Canadians. Fit in with the Anglos and be good citizens, get some education and a good job, and this probably drove my father around the bend. He lived bitter and died young. He was still in his fifties."

"I see."

"I don't feel particularly Ukrainian. I'm not sure I ever did. I fled from that stuff when I was still a kid."

"I see. Are there any points in your career that you might consider high points, any—"

"Oh, yes. Making detective, as they used to call it. Becoming a plainclothes investigator, that was a huge step forward for me. It happened in 1975."

"Tell me more about this time."

"Well, I'd been a cop in uniform for what, almost ten years. And I really wanted to move on. As a cop on the beat, I always wanted more of a challenge. I guess I was ambitious, but it was more a question of keeping things interesting, learning more about investigating, following a case right to its conclusion. And as a cop on the beat, I guess I was a bit of a malcontent."

"Like your father was?"

"Well, maybe. But when I finally became a plainclothes guy, and I joined up with Major Crimes, I can tell you, there never was a better job in all the world. Sometimes the politics of the job, on the force, at city hall, they could get on your nerves. Sometimes I didn't agree with my superiors. But I could ride with things good or bad as long as I got to do that job."

"Can you give me an example of what that job meant to you? An old case, perhaps?"

"Well, my first big case was back in the summer of 1978. A girl was missing, a nine-year-old girl."

"Would that be Melanie Pegg?"

"Melanie Pegg, good memory. Now, this case, like so many in this town, turned on a coincidence. In a big city, things can get complicated. In a small city, things tend to coincide, and what you have to do is keep your eyes open for the way the facts of a case might coincide."

"I see. And the Melanie Pegg case, if I recall, took rather a long time to investigate?"

"Yes, it did. Early on it went cold. The girl had been on her way to a community centre, a school in Nutana, where she did sports and gymnastics one night a week. And she didn't show up. The parents were distraught, of course. Divorced couple, so I had to interview them at different times, and they both co-operated with the investigation. The mother recalled that on this particular night, Melanie set out for the school with her badminton racquet. Anyway, the mother and father got involved with a drive to put up posters of the girl all over the city. Last seen carrying badminton racquet to this particular school. But there were just no leads. No body. No one had seen the girl that night, no signs of blood or violence, no strange vehicles reported, so things went cold and I moved on to other cases.

"Well, back then, I used to drink in some real dives. That's another story, I suppose. And one place I used to drink was just off Market Street, an establishment called the Harrington. The place has since shut down. I was alone, perhaps waiting for a friend to show up, I don't remember. I was drinking next to this fellow who kept trying to sell things to me. *I got it in the parking lot,* he kept saying. It seemed to me that he was either selling hot goods, or he was trying to lure me into a mugging situation. *I got it in the parking lot.* So finally I gave in. Why not find out?

"The man had a big rusty van. It was filled with bar bells, stereo equipment, speakers, oh, some golf clubs, a motor for a boat, an exercise bike, a metal box filled with tools and lots more. It seemed likely that this fellow had broken into some guy's apartment and cleaned him out. I didn't want to bust the guy, not while I'd been drinking, so I managed to get his first name, memorized his license plate, and the boys downtown brought him in. I came to work the following week, and they were going through the booty to find out who this stuff belonged to, and there was one article, just one article, that had a name on it. M. Pegg."

"My God, the racquet."

"Yes. So I interviewed the burglar myself, and I told this fellow it was a murder investigation. I told him that, at the bar, I had been tailing him, which of course was a little white—"

"Of course."

"And before I could even ask him how he'd gotten hold of the racquet, he broke down and confessed to the B and E, and he took me and my partner right to the place he'd broken into."

"The father?"

"The father. We hauled him in, reminded him of his right to counsel, but as usual he waived it. In our other interviews with him, he had never asked for a lawyer, so this time, I guess he didn't want to draw any attention to himself. In fact, he didn't have a clue why we wanted to interview him again. So we went over his previous testimony with him, sounded like routine stuff, and we asked him if he'd maybe forgotten to tell us anything. Like where he really was the night of his daughter's disappearance."

"Well, I'm right in front of him on a wooden chair, almost knee to knee. He's on a chair with rollers, and he begins to back away, and I think to myself, *I've got you now, you sonofabitch.*"

"Go on. Mr. Shmata."

"Could I change that?"

"What?"

"The sonofabitch part."

"Yes, of course. Carry on."

"So, I said to myself, aha."

"Aha?"

"Something like that. I said to the father, *If you weren't in the company of your daughter that night, how did you get hold of her badminton racquet?* I brought out the racquet and showed him. We'd gotten the wife to identify it first. Well, suddenly he was having fits. *Where'd you get that? Did you people break into my place without a warrant?*"

"*No,* I said to the guy. *We had help.*"

"And all from a little coincidence in the bar."

"All because things just decided to coincide."

"Do you ever use the term synchronicity?"

"Synchronicity. I've read about that but I forget what it means. Isn't that just coincidence with a B.A.?"

"Hah, I think I'll keep that. Synchronicity, as I understand it, is the coming together of two or more things that, initially at least, were unrelated. I think it points to a higher order of reality. Things can be *merely a coincidence*. But things are never merely synchronous. Isn't that thrilling?"

"I'll stick with coincide, if you don't mind. But seriously, when things come together in a case, it just feels like luck. Can you go back to calling me Bill now?"

"Do you prefer Bill or William?"

"William for interviews, Bill for Joe's Lunch."

"Joe's lunch it is."

EARL'S PITCH

Saskatoon, first day of spring 2003

"Hello there, young fella. Yer mother in?"

The boy stared up at Earl as though he were part of a television show and then looked away. The youngster was stout, almost plump, and he held a shoe box next to his sweat shirt.

"You the paper boy?"

"Yep."

"Remember me?"

The boy looked back up at him and said, "No."

"I useta live at Mrs. Miller's, eh? Place your mother works?"

"I'll get her."

The boy strode into the house and disappeared. He called his mother and returned to the door. He said, "Are you the man who takes walks, like down to the river?"

"That's me, Earl Claney. You call me Earl. I useta be a paper boy too, yknow."

"Yeah?"

"Useta call it doin rags. You call it that?"

"No."

Julie came to the door and stared at him. "Jesus Murphy," she said.

Earl raised his hand. "It's not what you're thinkin," he said. "I'm just droppin by to say hi."

"Come in," she said. "It's chilly out there."

She led Earl into her living room where a game show was playing on the television set. She snapped off the program. Earl hesitated at the entrance, taking in the objects Julie lived with every day, the sofa, which was bathed in orange light from a table lamp. The red and green pillows, an easy chair, a throw rug. A bright porcelain tiger that stood on a stand by the front door. Sammy was on the floor with three shoe boxes.

"Come come come."

"I'm just—"

"Come here, right in, that's it. Don't mind the mess."

"You look okay to me."

"I meant the house."

Little Sammy returned his attention to his shoe boxes, which were stuffed with cards of some kind.

"This here is Sammy."

"We innerduced ourselves. I bet you think I'm lonely or somethin."

"No, Earl, I don't think you're lonely." Julie returned to perch on the chesterfield. "Sit."

Earl made his way slowly past Julie and Sammy and lowered his tired body into the easy chair. It was a pleasure so deep it caught him by surprise. Sitting in Julie's living room was nothing like sitting in the King Eddie. It was a sober pleasure, a quiet pleasure. Every time he drank at the King Eddie, it seemed he was competing with his buddies for a share of the conversation, out-yelling them, out-laughing them. The more he drank, the more he spilled his guts. Earl was tired of spilling his guts to a bunch of drunks just to keep up with them.

"Nice little house you got here. You have a finished basement?"

"Kind of."

"How many rooms upstairs?"

"How did you get over here?" asked Julie.

Earl shifted on the sofa and groaned. "I'm the first livin human being in history to excape from Mrs. Miller's alive, an you wonder how I got here? Hell, I walked."

"You walked all the way from your place clean across Thirty-third?" said Julie.

Earl nodded.

"So," she said, "I know your phone don't work. Is your house still there? You got everything turned on again? You got heat an water?"

"Nope."

"No? How do you stay warm for God's sake?"

"It's the first day a spring, Julie. Who needs heat an water?"

"Earl?"

"Last few nights I bin sleepin at the King Eddy."

Julie swore softly, got up, shuffled into the kitchen. She was wearing pajamas and an old robe. Earl could hear her filling the kettle for tea.

"Thought you'd get me a beer," he yelled. "Guess I was mistaken."

Sammy looked his way warily.

"So, young fella, what do you like to do? You a baseball player? No? You play hockey? You sparkin the young gals yet?"

"I collect things," said Sammy.

"Oh?"

"Yes. And I like to read things."

"What things?"

"I like to read about submarines. And I read about magic. I know things about magicians."

"Gonna show me some tricks?"

"I don't *do* magic. I just read about it."

Earl relaxed into the soft cheap brown fabric of Julie's easy chair and began to breathe more easily. It had been a long walk to Julie's house. He'd had to stop and sit down on the curb several times to rest.

"What sorta things do you collect?" he asked.

"Just things. Stuff." Sammy continued to look warily in Earl's direction. "I don't do it all the time."

Earl guffawed at the boy. "Oh, that's good," he said. "I'd hate to think you done it all the time. Cause if you done it all the time you'd be what? A fulltime stuff collector?"

The boy said, "I collect sports cards and stamps in these boxes, and I collect model tractors and stuff in my bedroom."

Julie returned to the living room. "Earl, seriously, you want a beer?"

"Tea's fine."

Julie turned to Sam. She pointed to a bare spot on her wrist where her watch usually rested.

"Off you go."

Sammy turned to face Earl. "I can tell you who scored the most playoff goals of anyone."

"I said, off you go."

Sammy groaned, rose to his feet, and went up to Julie. He whispered something into her ear. Then he carried his shoe boxes off to bed. Julie brought out two mugs of tea, Earl's with milk and sugar. She had remembered.

"Sammy wants me to ask you to bring all your stamps here from now on."

"Tell him I'm good for it."

"You serious about what you said?"

"Huh?"

"You been sleepin in the King Eddy?"

Earl nodded. "That bastard's after me," he muttered. "I know it."

"That guy Shmata? He was back to the house again. Is he a cop? Earl, tell the truth. Are you runnin from the law?"

"Never mind. I don't wanna talk about it."

"You *like* sleepin in that fleabag?"

"It's not a fleabag. Feels more like home than Mrs. Miller's ever did."

"You still haven't told me why you can't sleep in your house."

Earl stared at his mug of tea. "That boy a yours. Sammy? I'll bet he could also use a stamp album for them stamps."

"He'll do just fine without one."

"Bet I could lay hold of a book on submarines."

"That's nice of you, Earl, but—"

"Look, you know what, I shouldn'ta come over so unexpected. You probably want to hit the hay."

"You got something on your mind, Earl. I can tell."

"I do not."

At last Julie offered Earl a cigarette and they both lit up.

"Them people that went an burgled your house, is that what's worryin you?"

"It was kids that done it," said Earl. "Anyway, I don't want to talk about it. I can't go back there. Can't go back to Mrs. Miller's neither. Me an the King Eddy, we were made for each other."

"Till your money runs out."

"Or till I run out."

"Jesus, I forgot to ask," said Julie. "You heard from the doctor?"

Earl nodded.

"And?"

"Oh, my ol friend is back. My tumor. Not huge or nothin, but it's growin some. Gal on the phone, she says they want me to come to the clinic for more tests."

"Of course they do, Earl, an you better go."

"Oh hell."

"I mean it, Earl, you better get your ass back there."

"Julie, I gotta get my affairs in order."

Julie's hand paused, the cigarette burning midway between her lap and her mouth.

"I got a house I need to sell, a few bucks in the Credit Union. Tidy sum. Twenny-nine thou give or take. Left over from the... you know."

"The Lotto Forty-nine."

"Yeah, an some other stuff."

"That's a good thing too, Earl, because you'll need every penny. Especially if you keep on stayin at the King Eddy."

Earl turned to look at Julie. She was blowing smoke up at the ceiling, and she would not look Earl's way. No room for pity in this place, he thought. Maybe that wasn't such a bad thing.

"How'd you like to inherit the money from the house, Julie?"

"You're outa your mind."

"All the money from the house an whatever I don't blow at the King Eddy."

"Do you think me an Sammy need a handout? Is that what you think? Because if it is, I can tell you: we done fine up till now and we'll keep on doin fine thank you very much."

"My, Julie, but you've got a temper."

"What're you thinkin of, Earl? Jesus."

"I'm not long for this world, Julie. I need to leave it somewheres. I can't just give it to my drinkin buddies, it wouldn't do no good. They'd just piss it away. But you. You've got a kid to raise."

Julie shrugged.

"You're sure. About the tumor."

"Damn right I'm sure. I can go do their tests an all that nonsense, but sure as we're sittin here I'm not gonna see too many weeks before I go funny in the head. Fits an blackouts an all that fun an games."

They were silent for a moment and finally Earl tapped some ashes into his cup and glared at the porcelain tiger next to Julie's front hall.

"You know, someone hung your inside front door silly. You need to hang that door proper."

"What about another operation?"

"Be the same thing as last time. They can't get at the whole thing, they can only get part of it."

"Is that just guess work or did a doctor tell you?"

Earl threw up his hands and let out a very theatrical sigh. "I need someone to leave my money to. Got no kids."

"You've got a sister. You told me you've got a sister somewheres."

"I got a sister in Edmonton. She married a contractor, so she's all right. An I didn't say there wasn't no strings attached, now, did I."

"So," said Julie, looking weary.

"That husband a yours. Does he still pay any bills around here?"

"Hah."

"I heard about the bastard," said Earl. "Mervy Carlin."

"You did, did you? Didja hear about the shotgun? Hey?"

Earl brightened. "I did. I heard all about the shotgun. I heard it was one a them goose guns."

"Ten gauge."

"No kiddin. Where'd you get your hands on one a them monsters?"

Julie told him about the Saskatoon Collector's Show and a fellow there who didn't require any paper work. He sold her a box of shells as well, an old fellow eager to get to know Julie a little better. He showed her how to load the gun, where the safety was, how to pull back the hammers, and which trigger to pull first.

"Mervy come home from the rigs. He was all tanked up and he come at me and I hauled out the howitzer."

Earl was all ears. "You are one dangerous gal."

"I told him I'd blow...somethin off. Somethin below the belt, and he believed me. He had no idea if the gun was even loaded."

"Was it?"

"Damn rights it was loaded."

"Jeeesus."

"Happened three years ago. Thank God Sammy was in bed. He never heard a thing."

"What a gal you are, Julie."

"You mentioned some strings attached?" she asked.

Earl took a deep drag from the last inch and a half of his butt and slowly exhaled.

"You quit yer job at Mrs. M's, you take care a me. I maybe got a few months left. Right this week I list the house. Soon as she's sold, you get the money. Mum's the word. No one nowhere hears about where I live. I'll be your secret boarder."

"Sounds like a proposal to me."

"Hah."

"Earl, if you're runnin from the law, you can tell me. I mean we gotta talk about these things."

"You might say I'm runnin from a whole buncha stuff, includin the grim reaper. I can't spill my guts, Julie, because quite honestly I just don't know where to start. Mind you," he said, remembering his nights of frantic conversation at the King Eddie, "if you went an got me drunk, you might just get an earful."

She glanced warily at him, without love or resentment, as though he were no longer just her friend or her charge, but a particularly vexing problem to solve before she went to bed. He remembered an expression she used over at Mrs. Miller's.

"I know what you're thinkin," said Earl. "When spring returns, all the squirrels come out to play."

Julie glared at him, nodding, as though all of this unique mess was somehow familiar territory to her, as though with one word she could summarize her life's greatest burden.

"Men," she said.

PART III: SPRINGTIME IN THE ROCKIES

TALES OF HOCHELAGA

Banff, late March 2003

"He doesn't live in Banff?"

"Ya-ya."

"I don't mean Banff Park, I mean the Banff townsite."

"Ya-ya."

Shmata and his driver were on a gravel road that ascended up a mountain in a series of sharp turns through a forest of pines and boulders surrounded by banks of grey melting snow. The man took it slow around each turn. He was driving Shmata to meet Wilhelm Grussen. He claimed to know Willie better than anyone in town, that he had even worked with him back in the fifties. At that time the Hochelaga was a hotel run on a European model: string quartets in the evening, Swiss alpine guides, no shopping mall in the lobby. The touring car in which Shmata was riding was a vintage black Chrysler that purred like a giant cat. In this car, on this assignment, Shmata felt as though he were drifting back to the radio days of 1951. Satchmo and Crosby crooning about the cool cool cool of the evening. Edgar Bergen and Charlie McCarthy, a ventriloquist with a dummy on radio. Nowadays, people had stuff, but not back then, at least not in Vegreville. You could see cars like this one, but it was a simpler, rougher time...

...Flat-tops and zoot-suiters fighting outside the Legion Hall. His father at the barber shop, drifting into disenchantment and insolvency. His mother, once the prettiest girl in Mundare, cleaning Anglo houses. And Joe Claney gets a summer job washing dishes in the mountains. Where one Wilhelm Grussen also worked, as a bellman.

Grussen had been tricky to contact. Shmata had phoned the number in Bertha's file, and a woman with an accent, apparently Willie's dispatcher, had answered. At first she claimed not to know the man, but Shmata must have lucked out, said some of the right things. She grilled him for a while, and then she arranged the rendezvous with Shmata's driver.

Shmata looked out the back window of the Chrysler. He could no longer see any buildings.

"Is this Grussen character some kind of a recluse?" he asked.

"Could be," said the driver, shrugging.

They crawled farther up the mountain, taking each hairpin turn so slowly that the tires raised no dust on the gravel. They had probably just left the town limits of Banff, but that seemed a world away from this forest full of melting snow. At last the car turned into a long rutted driveway that wound through the pines to a two-storey stone house. It looked like a government building from the era of the twenties, all slate, stone and mortar, several shades of grey, as though the house were built from the leftover materials at the construction site of the Banff Springs Hotel. A wisp of woodsmoke drifted from the chimney.

"You're sure this Willie still lives up here?" asked Shmata.

The man turned around in his seat and burst out in a high raspy giggle.

"I am this Willie."

Down in Banff, the old fellow had given him another name, an improbable one that Shmata had trouble pronouncing, and now the fellow was wheezing like a band saw.

"You are Willie Grussen?"

"I don't tell you nothing down there," the man said, waving a hand in the general direction of the Banff townsite. "I wait until I get some kind of feeling about you."

He was a heavy-set, rotund old man with a wide bulging face and a snowy white mustache like the hair on a pushbroom. He had never mastered the 'th' sound, so his words came out as *de, dis, dat, dem, dey*. He invited Shmata to come inside and meet his wife. Shmata was gazing up at the imposing structure of the house, perhaps an inn in its earlier life. It had a well-worn sign above the front door and two words gouged into the wood, painted red.

"*La Bohème.*"

"Ya-ya."

They went into the front hallway, and Willie Grussen turned on a few table lamps and a big chandelier to dispel the gloom inside. The place was on a ninety-nine-year lease, he told Shmata, and it had about twenty years to go.

"Then we got to give it up. That's okay," Grussen added. "This place has a longer lease than we have."

The interior appeared to have been a renovation site for some time. There was sawdust all over the floors and sawhorses set up for various power tools. Willie beckoned Shmata to join him in the kitchen, where he put on the kettle for tea.

"Lovey!" he cried up the stairwell, and a woman's voice answered back.

"So, Willie," Shmata began. "Those two bellmen. Lamont Spencer and Bishop Montgomery. You remember them?"

"Bish Montgomery, ya. They call him Bish."

"That was over fifty years ago."

"Some things I remember like jesterday, some things jesterday I forget forever." Willie tapped his head. "I forget where I put my measuring tape last night, but I remember what the girls look like in Aachen."

"How did you hear about the murders?"

"In the paper. In the *Herald*. I see their pictures and maybe it ring a liddle bell, I see their names *unter* the pictures, I remember who they are chust like that." Willie Grussen snapped his fingers.

"After more than fifty years?" said Shmata.

"You don't forget Bish Montgomery and the other guy. Spencer. A real couple operators, ya? A couple of *Krummstabbe*. You see? I remember this juiceless word *Krummstabbe* but I can't remember the English word."

They settled on swindlers.

"They had us all dancing to their chig."

"How do you mean?"

"I already was a bellman. It's only in the last ten years or so I become a tour driver. Back then I work with these guys in the summers." Grussen cleared his throat and thought for a moment. "You see, Shmata, we got the insiders and the outsiders. Everywhere we go in the world, insiders and outsiders. These two guys were insiders wiss a capital 'I.' They spend their lifes to make sure we all know the difference. They don't give a chit and they run the show. They were chust summer employees of the Hochelaga, but they run their own liddle show. Their daddies, you see, Shmata. Old families, lots of moneys, so they don't worry about the things the rest of us worries about."

"What was their own little show?"

Grussen held out one hand and rubbed his thumb across the fingers. "They control the tips each week, and some guys make big moneys on the tips. They cut out some guys, they cut in other guys. Spencer is the bell captain. You got to play by Spencer's rules or you don't get paid. And him and Bish, they run the card games."

"You didn't like these two very much, did you," said Shmata.

"Like them?" said Willie, after a pause. "These guys had all the answers. I am a goddam immigrant who speaks German only when no beeble are listening. Ashamed to speak German in public. I tell everybody I'm Swiss. That's how I get the chob. Spence and Bish, they had the power and I had to better myself. They knew I needed them. They were my lifeline."

"But you make them sound like con men."

"Oh," says Willie, "they come from good families, they got fine manners, they smile and everybody is heppy so long as you don't cross them. I was like the butler for these guys."

He went again to the stairwell. "Lovey!" he cried.

Again, a woman's voice answered. Shmata sipped his tea and began to relax into one of Grussen's rocking chairs, enjoying the novelty of a rocking chair in someone's kitchen. He let Grussen ramble on about the late forties and early fifties and how things were done at the Hochelaga.

"These parties," Shmata said, "in the staff headquarters."

"Buena Vista," said Willie. "We bellmen, we all got okay rooms, but Bish and Spencer, they got to live in cheesuschrist penthouses. Big living quarters like a luxury apartment, lots of space, and the steam queens, the girls who work in the laundry, do all their clothes for them. What a setup."

"Were the poker games a pretty regular affair?"

"Ho boy." Willie's face took on a look that bordered on nostalgia. "Sometimes they get pretty high stakes, ya, pretty high stakes. Guys go in there, lose all the tips for one month, lose hundreds of dollars. And in those days, Shmata, you drop a few hundred bucks, you really lose your shirt. Remember, Shmata, to Spencer, this is peanuts. Nothing. But to the rest of us, this is big potatoes."

"Were the games, you know…"

"Yaya. Crooked like the dog's hind leg, Shmata. Lamont Spencer and Bishy, they control the game so they could choose their victims.

They get one guy but not another, ya? You play crooked but you don't get your own guys. You go for the new guy or the outsider. You set him up like a target."

"And Joe Claney was one of their targets?"

Willie Grussen smiled like an evil dwarf.

"How did that all happen?"

"You know, Shmata," said Willie, "this is a secret for a long time."

"I understand."

An old woman swept into the kitchen, short and round. She beamed a mawkish smile at Shmata, and he rose to greet her.

"Play, play, Grussen!" she cried.

Behind him, Willie was inserting a tape into a boombox. Suddenly the kitchen was flooded with polka music. When he turned to face Willie's wife once more, she had her arms extended as though to hug him.

"Dancing?" she said.

"No, Lovey, you don't have to."

Shmata found himself bouncing around the sawdust-covered floor, swinging wildly past a table saw. A moment earlier, he was getting the goods from Willie, now he was dancing with the man's wife—no doubt the dispatcher on the other end of the phone who had set up this interview. It was four o'clock in the afternoon, and he was dancing with this merry redfaced beachball of a woman. And they were all sober! He couldn't wait to tell Letourneau about this. The things investigators did to get information. The polka lasted for what seemed to be a very long time, and Lovey and Shmata were gasping for breath in the sawdust-laden air, her husband coughing and applauding. The only thing missing to complete the picture was a bottle of shnapps.

"You come up to my house, you dance with my wife. We got rules around here, Shmata."

After a second mug of tea, Shmata asked Willie, "Do you remember who did the dealing on the train when Joe Claney lost? Was it usually the same guy?"

"Bish Montgomery."

"And was Montgomery, you know, a bit of a cellar man? A mechanic?"

"Oh ya. He was a mechanic all right. But old Bish, he don't deal from the cellar."

"No?"

"He's not a cellar man, he's a number-two man."

Shmata sat up in his easy chair and placed his empty mug back on the table. "A number-two man?"

"Ya, he don't deal from the bottom. No good to deal from the bottom. You can't see no marked cards from the cellar, Shmata. A number two man, he can deal the second card from the top without nobody sees him do this. And if he does it this way, the dealer gets to see his options, hm? He can give Spencer or himself all kinds of cards."

"Did Joe Claney get wise to Montgomery?"

"Ya, it was already the first game of the year, on the train to Bempf. Claney, he get real suspicious. Bish leaves the club car to see what's up with this guy Bulger. You know who I mean?"

"I do," said Shmata.

"A pathetic man."

Willie shook his head and glanced furtively at Lovey, who was boiling more water for tea. "I get to know him pretty good. Ex-navy, tall guy wiss liddle eyes. We tolerate each other because we are the outsiders, ya? We both get the bellman chob because this new manager, he don't like the oldboys league. The rich boys' league? Anyway, when Claney is losing his bundle, Bulger is off somewhere in the train. There is this screaming and yelling from the ladies' restroom."

Shmata nodded, looked up. Lovey was shaking her head at something, muttering.

"They play without Bish, and Joe Claney, he wins a few hands. Bish comes beck, he gets the deal, and for Claney it's game over, he loses everything. Oh, Claney, he knows something is up. He knows. He's dead broke for godsake."

"And Bulger was in the women's can?"

Willie stared ruefully. "He's up to no good with a girl on the train."

"Bulger was a bad actor, wasn't he. By the way, I gather that he died in prison."

"Derapist? Dead?" croaked Lovey, on her feet and ready to explode. She muttered some words in German and Willie smiled very sadly, nodding his head.

"Ya ya," said Willie, and passed a finger across his throat. "We are through with him, Lovey, ya? You hear already what he said. He's dead."

LUCK

Willie turned to Shmata. "He was such a loser, so pathetic, I almost feel sorry for the bested. I know, he was a goddam rapist, a violent sadistic man. He takes the girls off somewheres, threatens them, and he gives it to them. Even Bish, he tells him no-no for his way with the girls. Later on, when the trial comes, we find out he's done already time for this. But before Bulger goes to trial for Claney's murder, the other guys we work with, they say boys will be boys. The guys they have their needs and all that chit. That's how it was beck then, Shmata. And the girls, they never blows the whistle, until that summer."

"One of his victims blows the whistle?"

"Yaya. It was Lottie, the nurse's assistant, that girl in the train. She was the one."

"She blew the whistle on Bulger, did she? Were any charges laid that spring?"

Lovey nodded and Willie smiled sadly. "Nobody arrest this man for this attack because you see, Shmata, it was the *attempted rape*. The cops, later on, they tell her, if Bulger don't get convicted for the murder of Joe Claney, they get him for attempted rape. But she nailed him. She tells the manager for the hotel, and Bulger gets fired. They want him chust to go home, but he goes over to the Grayline office to be a driver, and Bulger gets a new chob. But this time he behaves himself, Shmata, and he never puts a hand on Lottie no more."

Shmata glanced over at Lovey and he decided to try some fishing. "She must have been a little bit braver than the others," he said.

"You betcha my life," said Lovey.

"The German nurses," said Willie. "They make them tough like Indian rubber, ya?"

You? Lottie? Shmata almost said it out loud to Lovey.

She gave an affirmative nod.

Something was about to make sense here, something Lovey had said. Or something was wrong here, or beginning to connect. A connection was forming for Shmata, forming, or about to fly out the window. He waited for the thought to come back. No luck. Connection dead.

Shmata stood up and began to pace around the kitchen. Suddenly he wanted a drink. It was not a fierce craving, more like a friendly old habit, and therefore all the more insidious.

113

"Willie, how did you get along with Claney?"

Grussen thought for a moment and rubbed his moustache back and forth. "I think I don't see much of Claney. He's in the basement of Buena Vista with all the rabble, I am at the top with all the princes. But I talk to him when I can. I think then he was an okay guy. Now, since he take our moneys, I still think this. A rough guy who could not hide his feelings about a person. He hated Montgomery and Spencer. Bulger too. But other beeble seem to like him, and he never gives me a hard time."

"I read in the trial transcripts where you testified about a fight between Claney and Bulger. That was before Claney stole the money, wasn't it."

"Ya-ya. Claney, he tries to give Montgomery a good licking. He knocks him down somewhere in the hotel. It must have been chust before Bulger gets the sack. Bulger he hears Montgomery cry out, he comes running and whecks Claney on the head. After that, it's like Bulger is glue to Montgomery. He's his big dog, ya? Even after he gets the sack from the hotel, he is still Bish's bouncer."

The need to have a drink was starting to wane.

Shmata made some notes. Much of what Grussen was telling him was not in the trial transcripts. When he looked up, Grussen was looking at him, so he asked Willie what he could recall about the murder of Joe Claney.

Grussen shrugged. "I remember it was because he stole the moneys. A big heist, ya? He had some inside information, I think so, from a waitress named Suzy. Bishy's old girlfriend I think. You know. She tells him where Bish and Spencer and us guys kept their moneys. And Bulger, he didn't lose nothing, but he was chust like a mad dog. You touch my master's money, I tear out your arsh-hole. They go together to Saskatoon, Bish and Bulger. I think maybe Bishy gets him to be the dog and go fetch, but maybe Bishy couldn't always control the dog?"

"But it was *all* of you bellmen that Claney wanted to rob?"

"In those days, Shmata, we all stick together. Spencer was the law, and we were his liddle deputies. Ya, Claney want to rob all of us. We were the guys on the top floor, Shmata. But Bish and Spence, he *really* wants to get them."

"Did you ever run into Joe's brother, Earl?" said Shmata. "After his brother got murdered, of course."

He muttered the name, shrugged, and changed the subject.

"I think I get Bulger mad at me forever at that trial. But the brother, I never heard nothing about the brother. What about this brother, Shmata?"

Lottie said something to Willie in German.

"Oh, cheesuschrist, Shmata. Ya, the guy who comes to the Hochelaga."

Willie had a brief exchange with Lottie.

"It was a long time later. It was not so long ago, ten years? In the early nineties. This guy comes to the Hochelaga. He tell everyone he wins the Lotto. He gets a good room and he gets drunk for breakfast lunch and dinner."

"*Bruder*," said Lovey to Willie.

"Earl Claney?" said Shmata.

They both nodded, and Willie raised an index finger and smiled. "This guy, this Earl Claney guy, he gets drunk, insults the waiters and the bellmen. He even takes a swing at me. He remembers me at the trial, he says. He's mad at me because I don't blow the vissel on Bishy. Ya, this brother, he stiffs the waiters and the bellmen every day, Shmata, but one night, drunk to his gills, he goes beck into the kitchen, he barges in there and he tips the dishwashers! He gives them, each one, maybe a hundred bucks!"

"It was the brother," said Lottie.

"Ya-ya, Lovey. And his brother Joe Claney, he was a dishwasher fifty years ago, Shmata."

He nodded, they all went silent, and at last Shmata rose to leave.

"No," he said to Grussen, "don't get up. I want to hike back to Banff."

"It's four miles, Shmata."

"But all downhill."

"Yaya, Shmata. Watch out for the bears in the bush."

Lovey walked him to the front door and smiled up at him. He handed her a card from the Hochelaga with his room number.

"We dance again, Shmata?"

"Ya-ya," said Shmata.

Shmata set off at a slow pace, yawning in the chilly air. Since his retirement from the force, and especially since his recovery from an operation for a malignant tumor in his gut, he had been walking a great deal. He was too old for running, too old for weights, but not too old to walk all over Saskatoon at the least excuse. He was fit in a sixty something sort of way. The early April mountain air was chilly but it would be good for sleeping, and as he eased his aging body down the gravel road to Banff, he began to mull over the conversation with Willie and Lottie Grussen. When Bulger's name was mentioned, she had leapt into the conversation with sudden ferocity. *Derapist? Dead?* she had cried.

Shmata needed a strong cup of coffee. He needed to wake up. He needed to think.

Derapist, as though Bulger had been some kind of purveyor of black therapy. Of course, he wasn't the therapist, he was the…

"Rapist," Shmata said out loud.

Halfway to the townsite, gazing up the valley at the Vermillion Lakes and the mountains cradling both sides of the river, puffing with every stride, Shmata woke up. It made no sense at all, it was merely another riddle. Nevertheless, he jogged the rest of the way to the nearest payphone in Banff.

EFFLUENT

Saskatoon, late March 2003

Bertha Eeling was up from her lair for the evening, but she hadn't yet gone home. She was showing Mike Letourneau how to access her most recently archived files. She had made a surprising discovery that somehow Letourneau had missed altogether. If he could discover this little gem on his own, with a little nudging from Bertha, he might become less of a Luddite and less dependent upon herself and the women who worked in the office. He towered over her in his new sports jacket as she sat in front of his computer in Major Crimes.

"Now," she said, in her most pedagogical voice, "if you don't want to Google it, and just stay within our system, you type in 'annals,' like this, plink, right here."

"Do that again?"

"Here," she said, and pressed "enter."

"Okay, but why not just Google it?" said Letourneau, the irritation rising in his voice.

She was losing him. Bertha had known for some time that Letourneau hated computers and made no secret of it. He was even suspicious of younger investigators who spent more than a few hours per week at their computers. Malingerers all. Only recently had he learned to do a Google search, and damned if he was going to learn a faster way.

Bertha repeated the process, waited a moment, stood up from Letourneau's desk, and checked his sweaty face for signs of comprehension. Nothing.

"Do it your way," she said.

Letourneau re-occupied the chair and squinted at the screen. He called up the search engine and typed in a word. Behold, a naked woman baring her ass at him. In a lipstick red balloon above her head were the words, *I go squishy for men like you!!* Letourneau floated a balloon of his own at the screen.

"Okay, now what?"

"The word is 'annals.'"

"So?"

"You typed in 'anals.'"

Just as Letourneau and two other investigators erupted in laughter, his phone rang. Bertha turned to Frenchie Demain, who was looking her way, a schoolboy grin on his ancient mug. Bertha returned the smile. She never tired of looking at the old man, his mane of white curly hair, his wiry ancient body with the stoop of an old monk.

"See what I have to deal with?"

"Mikey's not your ideal student," said the old man. "I would of hated to be his school teacher, eh?"

"I'm all alone with a beautiful gal," Letourneau was growling.

He turned to Bertha, covering the speaker with his massive hand, and pointed to the phone.

"Shmata says hi," he whispered.

"Hi," said Bertha, waving to the phone, and wondered if she were blushing.

"The what?" said Letourneau.

"Mikey works too hard," said Demain. "You musta heard, his unit had to work on two homicides just this past week. And that there home invasion? He's got cases comin out his ears."

She nodded at the old man. He didn't seem to be worried whether Letourneau heard him or not. This was strange. Frenchie could get away with anything in front of Letourneau, whose grudges and bad temper were legendary around the station.

"He comes up here too often after supper," said Frenchie, "when he oughta be relaxin at home."

"What about you?" asked Bertha.

"Oh, me, I prefer the night shift. Wife is used to it."

"You mean asshole's fax from Vancouver?" Letourneau roared. "*Therapist*, yeah. No, they never sent nothing else, just that fax. Squat. They got squat. Their guy from major crimes, he tells me they are *widening* their investigation. Remember that phrase?"

"You married too?" said Frenchie, pulling his mop from the roller.

"Me?" she replied. "Divorced. Long time ago."

"Just askin," said Frenchie.

"It doesn't seem to suit some of us," said Bertha, and wondered how many times she had repeated that same sentence.

"Shmata," Letourneau blared. "Listen to me for chrissakes. The bastard is dead. I told ya. Years ago. I don't know. So if he wants to nail the bastard why doesn't Montgomery just write fackin Bolger? *Maybe* he's forgotten. *Maybe*. So why, I mean if the bastard's dying, Shmata, why does he take the time to say the rapist. Why not just rapist? Anyway, it's all academic because like I say…"

Bertha and Frenchie both looked Letourneau's way. *The bastard is dead? Please God, she uttered to herself, let the bastard in question be Montgomery or Spencer or Joseph Claney and not who I think he means.* There was some real excitement in the air; it was coming in occasional squawks from the receiver. Bill Shmata was onto something. Letourneau looked her way and pointed to the phone, then dialed several circles around his own ear to indicate the state of Shmata's sanity.

"Which bastard died years ago?" she whispered to Letourneau.

"Bolger," he whispered.

"If you mean Bulger," she whispered back, "he is still alive."

Letourneau glared at Bertha as though she had struck him with a fence post.

"Hang on, Shmata. Will ya hang on?"

He clapped his hand over the speaker and turned to Bertha.

"What are you sayin?"

"Mike, I've just finished my Bulger section. Your office phoned the correctional people out in Vancouver yesterday. Cletis Bulger was parolled about three months ago. As far as I know, he's still—"

Bertha's voice was cut off by a long low moan of profanity, heavily laden with modifiers. Letourneau lifted his palm from the speaker and started to say something. Not a sound emerged from his mouth. He was exhaling like a fighter between rounds.

"Bill," said Letourneau at last, "it's me again. You at a payphone? Yeah, can you call me back in five or ten minutes?"

Letourneau put his index finger to his lips and ushered Bertha into his office adjacent to the Major Crimes section. He seemed to be cooling down with little success. He sat there a moment, held his head in his hands and slowly looked up.

"Alive?"

"Yes. Cletis Bulger is in Vancouver. I just found out. I was revising the last section of my file on him. He was parolled three months ago. Apparently he sees a parole officer once a month."

"And what? You decided not to tell me?"

"No!" she cried. "The reason I was showing you how to access my files was so that I could—oh, never mind. I wanted you to see it for yourself by going to the Bulger/Claney site." She paused. "You have no idea what I'm trying to explain, right?"

"Who gave you clearance to use my office to get information from the corrections people in Vancouver?"

"You did."

"Oh, right."

"Mike, is everything okay with you?"

"What the f—" Letourneau cut himself off in mid-profanity. "That's what Shmata was askin a few days ago."

Letourneau began pawing through some notes on his desk.

"And they said Bolger was—"

"Bulger. The name is Bulger."

Letourneau held up a notepad. "Well, a guy samed Sharma told me that…Bulger?"

"Yes."

"Bulger? Oh, shit."

Bertha went straight to Letourneau's computer and entered the name Bolger, retrieved some data, and then she did Bulger. The process took less than a minute. The first man had died in prison in 1999. The second had been parolled.

"That's classified stuff," said Letourneau.

"You gave me a code, remember?"

"I swear, Bertha, I swear."

"You swear?"

"I got a case a the stupids no doctor would ever believe."

When Shmata called again from Banff, Bertha listened as Letourneau attempted to extricate himself from the effluent he had become mired in. He chose to lean heavily, but not absurdly, on the listening skills of the man from India who had supplied him with the botched information.

"Yeah, yeah, Bulger sees a fackin parole officer once a month. What I'm getting at, Shmata…what I'm getting at…you think so…what you seem to have forgotten is there is so much discretion in our system you can send monkeys to Singsing. His last felony happened thirty-forty years ago. Killed an inmate while he was in the joint. The guy's, what, seventy-seven years old now? So he goes to a halfway house, he's in, he's out, he's up down an sideways through the system, and half the time even *they* don't know where the fuck he's gone to."

Yes, indeed. Letourneau had the stupids. He wasn't sleeping, one could tell. Once or twice she had seen him dozing off at his desk, and he flew off the handle at the smallest excuse. And quite possibly he had been flirting with her. Burnout, was Bertha's guess. She almost regretted showing Letourneau how to access her files by computer, because Bulger and the Claney brothers still somehow belonged to her. Perhaps she *had* been a bit stingy with her information.

"Yes, Shmata, I got it covered. The Vancouver boys will try to pick him up. I'll fax em right away. And we'll bring in Earl Claney just in case. And while we're at it, what about your little Kraut friend? How about—how ab—okay, okay, it was just a thought, Jesus."

Letourneau swivelled around on his chair to face Bertha again. Grinning sardonically, he made a duck out of his free hand and snapped the bill open and closed a few times.

"Okay, yeah, good. Yeah. I know. I know. God knows I know. Dealin with assholes, that's what. It's times like this I envy you, Shmata, freeloadin off in Banff, checkin out the ski bunnies. You still wanna come back part-time? I know, I haven't forgotten. Don't laugh. The boys upstairs just tabled a real nice package this week. I might just give it a second look. It would please our esteemed chief no end to see my ass outa here. Yeah. Yeah. You never know, Shmata."

"Here," said Letourneau, glaring at Bertha as though she too were a suspect.

"Me?"

"He wants to talk to you."

She took the phone. There was no doubt now: she really was blushing.

WILLIE REMEMBERS

Banff, late March 2003

For a man with a bladder and kidneys as old as Willie Grussen's, he drank too much coffee. And in spite of Lottie's disapproval, he sometimes drank it well after supper, and spent many hours reading and thinking when he could have been snoring in bed. Tonight was a strong coffee night.

Lottie chided him several times and then went off to bed. Willie would contend with the night in his own way, reading, nodding off, becoming owly-eyed and wakeful, and listening to the sounds of night birds and coyotes, or the occasional far-off roar of a spring avalanche. And he would worry about what he had said to William Shmata. Could it come back to haunt him in some way?

He had probably talked too much. He *always* talked too much. He could have told Shmata more, though. He could have told Shmata more about the trial. How Bishy and Spencer got the smartest lawyers around, just in case, and Bulger got a young man with a stutter, barely out of law school. Or that some of the stolen coins were from a valuable collection. Bishy's own father's coins! Willie was forming a new idea of how Bish and Spence had been killed. Perhaps the murders were committed by a business associate who had gotten a bad deal from them. Young bastards like those two, they grew up to be old bastards, and they made enemies.

Or perhaps Joseph Claney had had a son. Unlikely, because he was so young. But if the son of Joseph Claney had done the murders...

"Oh, Willie," he said out loud, "now you really dreaming up the bullchit."

But if a son had done the murders, it would be like the hand of Joseph Claney had reached out from the river and taken his revenge. Poetic justice. Spooky stuff. It seemed to Willie that the spirit of Joseph Claney was hovering somewhere nearby. And the ghost of bad old Bulger. Who could say otherwise?

Anyway, Shmata had his eye on Earl Claney. Let him harass this brother for a while. The man who won the lottery. Earl Claney would nurse the bigger grudge, and he could afford to have Bish and Spencer killed by someone else. Someone had been phoning around Banff to find Willie. Before Shmata had found him. Perhaps that man was this brother.

Willie wandered up to his bookcase. It had a couple of old covers draped over the books to keep the sawdust off. He parted the sheets and picked up a book. It was an English account of his own ancestors, the Sudetan Germans. He had been meaning to read it for some time, so he brought it back into the kitchen and sat where Shmata had been sitting a few hours before. He sipped his coffee and tried to concentrate. He mouthed the English words and realized that, some time ago, he had already read the introductory chapter. He flipped forward, he flipped back.

He couldn't concentrate, and not because of his uncertain memory for English words. He could not seem to keep the ghosts of Spencer and Montgomery and Bulger and Joe Claney out of the kitchen. They kept wandering onto the pages of his book. The one theme he managed to retain from the first chapter, however, was that the Sudetan Germans had had a proud history of resistance to tyranny. Resistance, *Widerstand*. This had always been a favourite word for Willie. If his people were endowed with the will to resist the tyrannies of the Third Reich, surely he too must have had it within him to resist the tyrannies that beset a man when he changed countries and started all over again. Lovey had the *Widerstand* in spades. She would never stay in a job if her employers treated her without respect. She had successfully resisted the threats of Cletis Bulger, who had promised violence if she blew the whistle on him. He had thrown a scare into her, so she threw one back at him, and he was fired and he left her alone. That was Lovey.

How did you resist the advances of Lamont Spencer, who could inspire a whole corps of impressionable young men to gather around him? How did you resist the entreaties of Bishop Montgomery, who made you feel like a somebody just by smiling at you in that approving way? Bulger used to dote on Montgomery like a puppy. The young fellow had him hypnotized.

Willie had come to Canada with a burning desire to fit in and become a somebody. He was tired of being pushed around, tired of political causes. He wanted to forget there ever was a war. As soon as he arrived in Canada, he became his own greatest cause. He landed in Montreal, went west, fell in love with the mountains, and conned the management at the Chateau Lake Louise into believing that he was a Swiss Alpine guide on a tour of the world. No one at the hotel had ever met a Swiss guide. But that hadn't worked out because, as he soon discovered, some of the well-heeled travellers he led up the mountain trails knew more about mountaineering than he did. So when he heard about an opening at the Hochelaga for a summer bellman, Willie jumped at it.

He remembered lugging his bags to the top floor of Buena Vista. When was that? Two summers before Claney was killed? The top floor was like a gentleman's club back then, a place where elite young people got together with other elite young people. And somehow Willie had conned his way into this playground, and into the magnetic field of Bish and Spencer, who wore the best clothes, went out with the loveliest young women, hosted the best parties, and strode through Banff and the high mountain trails like young princes. They were silly vainglorious little pups but they were the future. If he stuck with the little princes in the summer, showed them loyalty, with their family and social connections, they might take him into their circle, allow him to mingle with the rich and powerful. This was America (as he thought of it then), where social class was less important than it was in the old country. You could come from nothing and start over. Perhaps Bishop and Montgomery would offer him a chance to go back to Montreal and work for their daddies.

They never *said* that, of course, but it was easy to assume, especially if you had a burning hunger to better yourself. Nothing happened after the first summer at the Hochelaga, however, and Willie's dream began to fade. After the summer of 1951, when he and Lottie got together, and after the trial in Saskatoon, he never saw Bishop or Spencer again.

"Like a couple a little princes," he muttered out loud, and wondered if Lottie had heard him.

You could be born with *Widerstand* flowing through your veins, but with that fatal hunger, how could you resist the little princes who made you feel like a somebody? And all you had to do was demonstrate loyalty.

Cletis Bulger had fallen in with them for similar reasons in the summer of 1951. The manager was a real egalitarian. He had hired Bulger from the stack of blueblood applicants because Bulger had fought in the Big War. He came from nothing, he was barely out of jail, but the new manager didn't know that. Bulger got lucky just like Willie, and Bulger was desperately loyal. And now Bulger was dead as well. When. He should have asked Shmata *when*.

Oh well. Once in a while there was a guy who wouldn't play by the rules, who refused to be put down, and it wasn't Bulger. And it wasn't Willie. It was the dishwasher, Pillowcase, as they referred to him.

"*Verfluchte Kaffee,*" Willie said out loud.

He waited.

"Here it comes," he announced to the kitchen.

Massing in the dark, the memories descended, engulfing him, and he was back in bellman uniform again, with the gold and purple epaulettes and the brass buttons and blue pants, leaning in the doorway, listening to the two of them, the eternal fly on the wall. Hearing the news from the horse's mouth. *Come in, Willie, come on in. We're just having a little—*

"Come in," said Lamont Spencer.

He and Bishy were drinking whiskey in Spencer's kitchenette, a sombre twosome.

"Have a drink, Willie."

Lamont was pouring. He held the bottle in one hand by the bottom, leaning the neck precariously on the rim of Willie's whiskey glass. Bottom up, glass down. Amber splash. Glass up, bottom down. Everything Spencer did proclaimed his good breeding.

Bishop Montgomery looked very shaky.

Like the favoured pet in a new home, Willie Grussen padded over to the kitchenette window and kept his silence. Soon they would continue to have their conversation as though he weren't there. Willie sometimes preferred this invisibility they conferred on him. He watched Bishy, whose facial features rarely seemed to stray beyond an easy boredom. Today, however, something was different. Willie went back and closed the door.

"Poor mad bastard," Bishy murmured.

He held his tumbler with both hands. The icecubes jittered and tinkled like bells on a harness. He was drunk.

"What did he look like?" asked Spencer.

"He had a fat lip from the thingamee with Claney…he was very subdued. I don't think he wanted to talk. To anyone, I mean. He looked depressed. I mean, one would, wouldn't one."

"What did he say?" asked Spencer.

"It was like I wasn't even there."

"Bishy, did he say anything?"

Montgomery didn't seem to hear. He held his drink up to his lips and rubbed the rim of the tumbler back and forth over the cleft on his chin.

"I saw the whole bloody thing. I talked with the policemen while the fight was going on. I said I was there to try and stop Bulger and they swallowed my story. I can't believe we all just stood there."

Montgomery turned to acknowledge Willie, gazed at him with a weariness that was close to weeping, then resumed his account.

"Claney just threw the golf bag into the river, he threw the whole bloody thing into the river. Gone."

"Jesus."

"And then Bulger went King Kong, and they fought like animals. In full view of the police. Officer Salter was the fellow in charge. Bit of a milquetoast. Claney went down, he was barely moving, he yelled something, and Bulger heaved him up to the railings like a sack of mail, and then Bulger just…."

"Good God," said Spencer. "So it's true."

"Yes, of course. Bulger treated Claney like…"

Montgomery was wagging his hand at the stuffed mink on Spencer's bookcase just visible from the kitchenette.

"He went after Claney like he was a little rodent. Lamont, I have never seen such rage. I mean, all I wanted Bulger to do was to get Claney to give back our money."

"Bishy," Spencer said, "I hope I'm not being thick, but I still can't quite see this. You mean the officers in charge—"

"Yes."

"They just stood there?"

"Salter and his partner, Moore was his name, they seemed to hesitate. And they got to Bulger a second too late. Because, you see, Lamont, he saw them coming and picked up Claney like he was a…"

Again Montgomery pointed to the stuffed mink.

"Up and over."

"Jesus."

"Cheesus."

"Splash."

"Did Bulger say anything at all to you before they took him away? Any *words*, Bishy?"

"Yes, he said…as though he was only just realizing what he'd done. He told me—you're not going to believe this, Lamont—he told me Claney's last words."

"My God."

"Claney looked Bulger in the eye—this must have been just before he—"

"Yes, of course."

"Claney looked Bulger in the eye and he said, *I'll be comin back, asshole.*"

"I'll be coming back?"

Montgomery nodded.

"Strikes me Claney had a bit of an imagination," said Spencer, gazing at the stuffed mink.

They all sipped their whiskey.

"I think, you fellows, I think that I am going to get squiffed this afternoon. With your permission, of course."

"Permission granted."

"Lamont, we are, I think, in the clear. They believed me about trying to restrain Bulger. And I didn't tell them a thing. I mean, beyond the obvious."

"The police? You mean you didn't tell them about our money?"

"I told them about our money. How could I not? But I didn't tell them a thing about Daddums's precious coins, or our poker games. I told them it was all just tips. You know how things tend to get…all complicated when reporters close in."

Spencer opened his mouth the smallest amount to release a bubble or two, a perfect tiny corporate belch. "Yes, of course. It's one thing to play high stakes poker in the bellmen's quarters. But it's quite another…la-dee-dah etcetera." Spencer's hand fluttered up toward the window until the thought had flown away.

"To cheat at cards," said Montgomery.

Spencer was looking down at the floor.

"None of that, Bishy," he said. "Now, none of that." He turned to Willie for the first time. "Mum," he said.

"Ya-ya," said Willie.

"Oh, Bishy," said Spencer. "What a way to end our last summer in the mountains."

"Does this make us cads, Lamont?"

"Not in the slightest. This was inevitable. We tried to teach Claney a much needed lesson." Spencer brushed back his closecropped hair, adjusted his glasses. "Do you know what we tried to teach Claney? Where he belonged and where he didn't belong. That's all. He was a smalltime thug and he didn't belong with the big boys."

Montgomery looked quite miserable. Spencer picked up the bottle again, replenished their glasses.

"Well, I'm out a thousand plus, and you have lost your Daddums's prize coins. Twenty canes on the buttocks for you."

"Gone," said Bishy. "Bottom of the Sass-katchewan River."

"Claney, you mean?"

"Our money."

"Right."

"How on earth could I have known that they were *collector* coins? They were just lying loose in a canvas bag like any other silver. And I manage to get them all back, give or take a few, and Claney has to get greedy and spoil everything. Daddums will soon have my testicles dangling from the mantle in his study."

Willie peered cautiously at Montgomery and Spencer. All of a sudden they were laughing like crazy men, and their laughter went on for a good minute.

They both looked up at Willie, raised their glasses, as though to include him in their sentiments. But what do you say to a faithful pet? Montgomery fell into a staring contest with Spencer's stuffed mink, the sleek black creature he had won from Claney on the train. The taxidermist had managed to lever open the animal's mouth to produce the effect of a snarl. Perhaps the snarling mink reminded Montgomery of Joseph Claney. It certainly reminded Willie of Claney. Everywhere, on this day, the most improbable things would remind Willie of Joseph Claney.

"You know," said Montgomery, "on my way back east I'll take the same train Claney did? The same train where we took him for all his cash? I might even get served by the same waiter and get drunk at his favourite table. I tell you, Lamont…"

Bishop's ice cubes had resumed their nervous tinkling. He plopped his drink back on the table, clenched his fists, and bent down towards his lap, until his tanned face grew deep red.

"Easy, old fellow," said Spencer, twiddling between thumb and forefinger the cork from his bottle of scotch. "By now, Bulger has one of those…you know…dingy lawyers. We'll testify, if we have to, that Bulger was acting entirely on his own, and then Bulger will disappear into some faraway prison and we will go on with our lives. Bulger did this on his own."

"The hell he did," Bishy whispered.

"You know what I mean. We didn't pay him to…to…dump Claney over the bridge."

Montgomery was weeping and shaking. "And this trial, this fucking trial. People will say I put him up to it, which isn't that far from the truth. I tell you, Lamont, this whole awful fucking thing…it is becoming…*unbearable*."

Spencer waited until Montgomery had wiped his eyes, blown his nose and taken another gulp from his glass of whiskey. He tossed the cork from the bottle of scotch playfully at his friend.

"Good catch, Bishy. Now, think of it this way. There is nothing whatsoever the police can learn that would implicate Buena Vista in any way. If we have to, we'll get good lawyers to keep us out of this mess. And Bulger will not have a leg to stand on. But he'll get a fair trial. It's too late in the season for us to get the sack for running card games. You'll go back to Montreal—"

"I'm not going back to Montreal."

"You're not—"

"Daddums has arranged a little jobby for me. He thinks I should have stored his precious coins in the hotel safe and I didn't. I mean, how do you tell the scarce ones from the ordinary ones? I had better things to do. So, I'll be teaching youthful bluebloods English and racquets at

Appleby College in fucking *Oakville*. My atonement, you might say. It's either that or…"

"Yes, of course," said Spencer.

"What was Claney thinking when he told Bulger he'd be back?"

"One says the damndest things, I suppose," said Spencer.

Willie shrugged.

Bishop Montgomery was still clutching the cork from their bottle of scotch. He hurled it at the stuffed mink on Spencer's bookshelf. It missed, and the mink remained where it stood, snarling or smiling among the books…

Willie Grussen found himself staring at his own collection of books, mostly obscured now by the dust cover. The fire in the stove had gone out. It was getting chilly in the room. He lifted the dust cover and replaced his history of the Sudetan Germans on the shelf.

"Where are you, *mein Freund?* Where did you go?"

He threw back the dust cover a little farther to his left.

"Aha," he said. "Here you are."

And there it was, Willie's own little heist from the summer of 1951, a little moth-eaten, a little dusty, but still that same fierce expression on its face. More than a snarl, a bitter triumphant smirk.

"Good night Joe Claney," he said. "Wherever you are."

PART IV: THE DOG

THE PUSHY OLD MAN

Banff, April Fool's Day, 2003

Shmata was sitting in a plush chair in the manager's office, listening to the bustle of skiers in the lobby of the Hochelaga. This morning the wind was gusting, the snow falling and drifting all over the highway, cutting down on visibility. Most of the skiers were staying put, milling around, waiting for a change in the weather. Shmata had one more day left in his reservation, and because Letourneau's Resource Fund was paying for it, he thought he would do some leisurely poking around. Perhaps, after lunch, he'd take a walk into Banff and see the sights.

Right now he was breathing in the atmosphere of the Hochelaga. It had been built by some wasp businessmen from Montreal, who had named the hotel after the original name of their city. Shmata wondered what Montreal had been called before it was Hochelaga. At least two of Shmata's grandparents had come from the city of L'vov in Galicia. People were now calling it L'viv. When his grandparents were young, it was called Lwow, and before that, Lemburg, and before that, Leopolis. By tracing the name changes, you could tell who had ruled the city. The Austro-Hungarians, the Poles, the Russians, the Ukrainians, God knows who else.

The Hochelaga had had a facelift and been purchased by a new set of investors, and its official name was now the Beaulieu-Barzun Hotel of the Rockies, but everyone still referred to it as the Hochelaga.

The manager, Mr. Downton, and an older fellow breezed in, and Shmata rose from his chair. The older fellow was carrying a cardboard box from a Banff wine shop. Downton was carrying a tray with coffee mugs and biscotti. He laid it down on his own desk with such flourish that Shmata felt sure he had been a waiter at some time in his youth.

"Mr. Shmata, this is Jimmy McDade, our manager of the transportation desk."

They shook hands.

"I hear you've been talking to our Willie," said McDade. "Is he a suspect, then?"

"No," said Shmata, and he wondered why McDade would have thought so. "He never has been. But a long time ago, he had known the two men who were murdered in Vancouver."

"Yes," said McDade. "And the three of them were right here at the old Hosh. A bit before my time, I'm afraid." He stood before Downton and Shmata, his long arms dangling for a moment.

"So. You want to see some old photographs?"

"Yes," said Shmata. "Did you say, 'our Willie'?"

McDade nodded. "Oh, he doesn't work for us any more, but he's driven our guests around in that old limo for at least ten years. Before that, he was our oldest fulltime bellman. He'll never completely retire."

"If you'll excuse me," said Downton, "I have to ingratiate myself with the idle rich."

Downton bade them goodbye and dashed into the lobby.

McDade sat in Downton's chair with the cardboard box on his lap. His face was deeply wrinkled, like an old chamois, and he had a thick shock of white hair combed straight back from his forehead. His face was red, as though for some reason he felt perpetually embarrassed. Booze, Shmata noted. He had that look about him.

"Why would you assume that Willie was a suspect?" asked Shmata.

"I have a terrible habit of blurting things out," said McDade, feigning shame.

"Then you don't have any information at all? About Willie, I mean."

"No," said McDade. "Perhaps I said what I did just then because you're not the first person to come asking about our Willie."

"Another investigator has been here?"

"Well, I doubt very much if he was a detective. Why do you people never use the word detective any more? It's such a delicious word. Anyway, this fellow, he was certainly *butch* enough to be an investigator. Oh, dear, I've done it again, haven't I."

Miming the pose of a naughty boy, McDade placed the tips of his fingers over his lips and bowed his head.

"Where was I, oh yes. A fellow, an older fellow came through here, oh, maybe two weeks ago. And he said he was looking for Willie Grussen on a matter bearing on the investigation. His name was... oh, dear."

"It wasn't Bulger, was it?"

Jimmy shook his head.

"Cletis Bulger?"

"Bulger Bulger Bulger. No, not Bulger."

"Did he say *what* investigation?" said Shmata.

"No, he wouldn't say. But for sure, he was a bit long in the tooth to be a cop. A former cop maybe. If I had to guess from his questions, I'd say he could have been a former detective. I simply can't remember his name."

"What sort of questions did he ask you?"

"Someone must have told him that I knew Willie. And this fellow said, *Well, if he lives in town, why isn't his name and address in the phone book? Well, I don't know, you tell me. You say you still hire this fellow to drive guests? Well, how do you get hold of him?* The man was very pushy, especially for an old fart."

Shmata felt a shadow falling over their conversation in Downton's bright and cheerful office. He could feel the presence of the man they were groping for.

"What did you tell this old fellow?"

"Nothing," said McDade. "He gave me the creeps."

"I'm glad you didn't," said Shmata. "And how long ago did you say this was?"

McDade once more placed the tips of his fingers over his lips, but this time without ironic effect.

"It was on the morning after St. Patrick's Day. It was the eighteenth. I know it was the eighteenth. Because the night before Downy and I, I mean Jeremy, our esteemed manager, had gone into Calgary to an Irish pub…and we got into the Bushmills. To honour my ancestors, you understand."

"Of course."

"And I was on the desk the next afternoon with the purple icks, exhaling Irish whiskey on my guesties, and up came this pushy old fellow. *Mister McDade, I want an honest answer from you. When I say honest, do you know what I mean?* God save us. He was about—"

Jimmy interrupted himself, did a little yelp, and brought his hands together and smiled for Shmata.

"Claney. He said his name was Claney."

"Claney? Earl Claney?" said Shmata.

"No," said Jimmy.

"A short scrawny man, about sixty-five or so?"

"No," said Jimmy. "Not short or scrawny. And I'd say he was older than sixty-five."

A phrase in the fax from Vancouver was winding through Shmata's memory. *Don't fuck with Saskatoon.*

"Did he say his name was Joseph Claney? Joe?"

Jimmy thought for a moment. "I don't *think*...he gave me a first name."

"Good God."

McDade brought out some photo albums from the hotel's little archives. They went through several dozen black and whites from the 1950s, and at last Jimmy produced a group shot from July of 1951. Five bellmen in uniform were gathered with some friends on the steps of a large three-storey frame building. Shmata had seen the building, because he looked down on it from his room. It was called *Buena Vista*, and it had housed some of the hotel staff. Two of the bellmen had their arms around the same young woman, and her fingers had found their way around the young men's waists. One tall bellman, the only one with a cap, was smiling over his brood as though he were the father and they were his children. A haughty but tolerant half-smile.

Jimmy was running his index finger over the names penned in at the bottom of the photo. Lamont Spencer, the name at the bottom said.

Bishop Montgomery appeared to be drunk. He was so deeply tanned, he looked almost Mediterranean. He had draped his arms over two young chambermaids who seemed to be straining to keep him up. And the smiling Spencer, yes, his haughty smile was probably directed at Montgomery. Willie Grussen (obviously Willie, but looking very fit and rugged) was seated, and he was smiling apprehensively at the antics of Montgomery and the two girls.

Only one person in the group was not smiling, a fellow even taller than Spencer. He had a crew cut, very short and flat across the top, and he was dressed in Grayline shirt and trousers, a company jacket thrown over his shoulder. He seemed out of place, and instead of looking at anyone in the group, he was focused beyond them, beyond the photographer, as though he were watching for bears. He was the only one in the picture without a name.

"This man is very likely Cletis Bulger. I've seen his picture from when he was still in the navy. Could your pushy old man have been him?"

"Oh, deary me," said Jimmy. "I could not honestly say. He just looked at me with these intense eyes. *When I say honest, do you know what I mean?* He absolutely *ruined* my hangover."

Shmata made a call to Willie Grussen from his room in the hotel, and Lovey answered. A band saw was whining in the background. Lovey called her husband to the phone.

"Shmata," he said, "You are still here? You sound not so heppy this morning."

"I'm afraid your old friend Bulger is back in the land of the living."

"This is your April Fool's choke?"

"I'm afraid not."

There was a pause at the other end, and then a flow of German phrases that Shmata interpreted as incredulity, so Shmata gave a brief summary of his conversation with Letourneau the night before. "Bulger has been out of prison for three months," Shmata added, "living in Vancouver."

"Cheezus God."

"And some old fellow was here two weeks ago looking for you."

"Ya-ya."

There was a series of muffled sounds from Willie's phone, and finally two words in Willie's rasping whisper: *He's out.*

Right then, with those two words, *He's out*, Shmata wondered if Willie and Lottie's residence up on the mountain had been chosen deliberately so that they could never easily be found. Shmata's mind was bouncing around like clothes in a dryer. His strange dance with Lottie, who might have been frisking him.

Bertha's file, with all the extra notes. Earl Claney's small room in Mrs. Miller's. Bulger's vigilant gaze in the hotel photo. Letourneau's fractured account of a man and a golf bag plunging into the river. The fax describing how brutally the two men in Vancouver had been beaten. Claney's blue and white house.

Claney's blue and white house with the back door boarded up.

"Willie. Willie?"

"No news of Bulger since then?" asked Willie.

"None. He's being sought by the police in Vancouver. And I'm not sure if the fellow looking for you at the hotel here was actually Bulger. It might not have been Bulger. Willie?"

Willie was muttering to himself or Lovey in German.

"Willie, listen to me. When the brother, Earl Claney, came to the Hochelaga all those years ago, and got drunk."

"Ya-ya."

"Did he ever blurt out anything about the money his brother stole? Or any stolen money at all?"

For a moment Willie said nothing. He cleared his throat.

"That Claney, the younger brother. I am bell captain to the hotel, and he finds out who I am. That I knew his brother, Joe. Then he gets drunk at the hotel, and he yells me all kinds of chit. He tries to shove me, takes a swing at me. Then he yells out, before the cops come to take him away, he says, *I got all your tips*, he says. *All you high und mighty meatheads, I got all your tips, you candy-ass bozos.* Meatheads and bozos, something like that. He was mad as a goddam chithouse rat, Shmata, but somehow, he must know about this money."

"Why would Earl Claney want to visit you, Willie? Or Cletis Bulger. Was Bulger mad enough from your testimony at the trial to want you dead?"

"I don't think so, Shmata. But always I'm afraid for Lottie. I think he's not so keen on Lottie. And maybe he want to find out about the moneys, Shmata. Maybe he's suspicious that big bag don't really go into the river."

"But Willie, why would Bulger even care about a few thousand dollars worth of coins off in another city?"

"A few thousand, Shmata? *Ach*, then I forget to tell you."

"Tell me what?"

"These coins, the ones from Bish's room, they belong to his daddy. And his daddy is a big collector. Bishy steals them from the old man and Joe Claney steals them from Bishy. The old man, he tells Bishy, you get them back or I cut you off wissout a penny."

"And Bulger knew all that?"

"I don't know, Shmata, but maybe he figures this out."

Shmata was silent. Bulger was probably out there, an old rogue bear waiting to rush at its prey. It had to be Bulger, posing as Earl Claney. Or Joseph Claney. Whose body was never found. Whose presence seemed to be everywhere like a wakeful ghost. Perhaps Bulger, if it was Bulger, would be back to Saskatoon to settle a score and pick up the loot in the bargain. Perhaps he'd been the one to break into Earl Claney's house in late January. A little trip to Saskatoon between visits to the parole office in Vancouver, like the one he might have made here in mid-March. Perhaps Earl's body would soon be turning up in the same river where his brother was dumped over fifty years ago.

"Willie?"

"Ya, I'm here."

"Will you be careful?"

"Ya-ya, we can take care of ourselfs up here, Shmata. We got no listed address."

"He could follow you up there in a car."

"Shmata, you can't follow a guy up a road with hairpin turns, you should know that. Because the guy ahead of you that you are following, he looks down and he sees you coming."

"I see you've thought about this, Willie."

"The body gets old, Shmata, but the mind still ticks."

THE STUPIDS

Mike Letourneau hated typing up communications of any kind, he hated sending faxes, he hated any activity at all that involved paper work or computer screens. But goddam it, once in a while there were exceptions. This morning, for example, he was composing his return fax to the Vancouver Police Service. This message was overdue. Of course, he had sent a couple of messages during the interim just to reassure them that he had his best man on the job. Shmata, the sixty-one-year-old whiz kid.

Put your best man on it. The Saskatoon Police Service had a busy bunch of investigators, every damn one of them. Not like a certain detective, formerly of Saskatoon, by the name of Martin Steel, B.A. This weekend, for example, there had been a domestic homicide in Silverwood, a gang-related assault at a party on the west side, and an attempted murder on Market Street. The Major Crimes boys and the uniforms were stretched to the limit.

"Please find by sep. mail, transcripts sent from trial of Cletis Bulger for murder of Joseph Claney, plus our summary of our findings for period of…"

Letourneau looked up and gazed through the glass walls of his office. He wondered what Bertha Eeling might be doing down in her part of the building. He really should give her some credit for putting him straight on the facts of Bulger's release from prison…he really should give her some credit, but Letourneau was not entirely pleased with Bertha's manner of late. She used to show up once or twice a week at the office after supper to do some work. But only once in the past week or more. As the warmer weather progressed and the last of the spring melt was flowing into the gutters, Bertha had begun to hurry out of her office and drive home before he had a chance to gab with her, correction, flirt with her. Women acted funny when a new man was around, and Bertha was acting funny. But she didn't strike Letourneau as that sort of a woman, the type to go silly over a man all of a sudden.

If anything, she had her defences up in that department, which made it all the more…well…challenging, to flirt with her during the evenings when the paper work began to pile up. She was pleasant and helpful and almost goddam irresistible.

Bertha and Letourneau had a mutual assistance arrangement going. If he dug into the Department Anals (as he now called them) for her, pulling out old stories from the days when he was a rookie cop, she would write up some of his current files for him.

She had such a good mind for writing up reports, a no-bullshit style to her writing, that she made Letourneau look like a goddam college graduate.

"Where was I?" he said to his screen.

Where Letourneau was, was typing up his dynamite fax to the boys in Vancouver.

…enclosures would have arrived in Vancouver sooner, but me and my investigatory staff, no, Shmata and me, no, Special Investigator William Shmata and I, no…*our people*…had to do some checking re: investigations in Saskatoon and Banff. Should you need this in your own investigation…

"Hah."

…your own investigation, we have come up with the following information:

1) In your February fax to my office, you mentioned that Mr. Montgomery (vic #2) had no known enemies in Vancouver. We have discovered that both he and Mr. Lamont Spencer (vic #1) had one enemy in common in Vancouver dating back to time of murder trial referred to in my enclosures (enclosed). Suspect's name is Cletis Bulger. As you will see from trial transcripts, sent by separate cover, Bulger was convicted of the murder of Joseph Claney in 1951. Since his release from prison, he has been residing in Vancouver. (See info, below, re: parolee's address and particulars.)

As well, he was prosecuted for rape circa 1947 in Winnipeg, Manitoba.

Letourneau's two giant index fingers sought the keys of his computer and thumped out the words. He was humming, he was unstoppable. The words came fast and furious, and he realized with a sense of relief (and without an ounce of resentment) that he did not need Bertha Eeling to type his goddam communiqués. He went back and underlined a few key phrases *(Suspect's name is Cletis Bulger)*. He did this for emphasis, and not, as some would accuse him, for the sake of rubbing obvious facts in the noses of the Vancouver investigators.

"Where was I?" Letourneau muttered once again.

2) Theory of Primary Evidence, re: note left by vic #2: In state of crisis near death, with head trauma, etc., vic #2 (Montgomery) probably could not remember name of assailant. Assailant, however, was known to both vics from incidents arising from circumstances back in 1951-52 re: murder of Jos. Claney. In our opinion, vic #2 remembered that assailant had been prosecuted for rape. Therefore, message written down by vic #2, Montgomery, just before he died was probably "the rapist" (ie, Bulger). Note re: *Don't eff with Saskatoon,* this is possible red herring Bulger left to make investigators think perpetrator was someone in Saskatoon, ie, one of the Claneys.

3) Motive for recent double murders: Both Montgomery and Spencer in 1951 had sought to reclaim their moneys stolen by the late Mr. Jos. Claney. Bulger allegedly done their bidding. According to witness located in Banff, during summer of 1951, Bulger was their watch dog, bouncer at their poker games etc. At the trial Earl Claney claimed that Bulger had planned to kill his brother all along. Both vics agreed this was possible. Motive for both murders therefore revenge for being…hung out to dry? Na. Thrown to the dogs? Railroaded? No…revenge for being A-B-A-N-D-O-N-E-D.

Letourneau would have to get someone to check this over. Asshole Steel would be reading this at the other end, and he was sure to make snide comments about Letourneau's grammar.

4) Action recommended: Immediate apprehension of Mr. Bulger.

Letourneau looked up from his computer screen. He had a sore back. It came from the hunch he assumed every time he had to hunt and peck his way through a long communiqué. His large hands were better suited for applying hammerlocks or clubbing the surly fellows who resisted the long arm of the law.

Bertha Eeling, on the other hand, had long lean fingers that flew at a heartstopping rate over the keys. Beautiful hands. She and Shmata, he happened to know, had had lunch together on at least two occasions, and were known to have long conversations on the phone. He suspected that Shmata had the stupids for her. Of course, these conversations were business calls, but Letourneau was a bit uneasy at how eagerly they gabbed back and forth, exchanging information and bantering all the time. Surely to God, Bertha was not getting it on with sixty-one-year-old whiz kid Shmata. He was too goddamned old for her, it was disgusting to think about. No. Bertha might be seeing someone all right, but it wasn't Shmata. Of that he could be certain.

Because, he concluded, handing a copy of his communiqué to Angie, one of the better secretaries in Letourneau's section, Shmata just did not have a way with the gals.

"Check this over for me, wouldya sweetheart?"

Angie looked up at Letourneau as though he had just said, *Woman, run barefoot through my hair.*

He wondered why. Why, in the ordinary course of her duties, should Angie give him a sour look?

A moment of self-knowledge was coming out of its silo and about to be launched in Letourneau's direction, but one inward glower from Letourneau, and the mission was aborted.

MRS. MILLER TRIES TO HELP

Saskatoon, mid-April 2003

The groceries were all put away, the laundry machines were humming along, the beds made, the old ladies asleep, pooped and laundered and smelling sweet, the night girl doing the floors. Everything was in its place. Mrs. Miller would have gone home hours ago, but for the empty bed in Room Four. She had even managed to hire a new girl to take the place of Julie Belanger, who without warning had given her notice. But no one on her meagre waiting list, so far, had come to claim the empty room.

Earl Claney had clearly gone off the deep end. He claimed he was moving back into his house, but any fool knew that plan would go nowhere. He would have his independence again, and as soon as he went off to drink with his old cronies or skipped his meds and had another episode, he would be back in hospital wondering who he was. It didn't make a bit of sense.

The doorbell rang.

The doorbell in her mind also rang, it was just that sudden: *Earl Claney had taken up with Julie Belanger. She had bewitched the little fellow. She needed a meal ticket. That little slut was after his money.*

Mrs. Miller opened the door and looked up to see the face of a tall old gentleman. *Aha, she thought, Room Four is about to be filled.*

"Hello there," said Mrs. Miller with a bright smile. "Can I help you?"

"Maybe," said the old fellow.

"Come in, come in," she chirped.

"I was lookin for someone," he said.

"Oh?" she said, and felt her hopes foundering. "And who might that be?"

"Old pal a mine," he said, scraping his boots. He looked like a buffalo trying to dance. He kept staring at his boots as he moved them back and forth on the mat. Then he looked at her. He had big front teeth and he was gnashing his molars nervously back and forth. He might have been quite the fellow in his day. A shy old brute of a man with a big square head and small jerky eyes.

"Name of Claney?"

"Oh, yes," she said. "He was one of our guests. Earl Claney. He moved out. You didn't miss him by much."

"Well, darn it," said the old man. "I've come all the way from out west," he said.

"Come right in, Mr. ah, come right in. I didn't get the name."

"I never give it, did I," he said, and then he smiled like a real reprobate, all teeth.

This one was playing his cards close to his chest. What the heck, she might just give him a try.

"Would that be Alberta?" she said.

The big fellow sat down heavily on one of Mrs. Miller's sofas. He looked like he belonged there. She wondered if he could afford to live at her home. She couldn't really tell from the clothes he was wearing. He didn't seem the executive type. He wore a black hooded car coat with wooden pegs for buttons. It made him look like an old sailor.

"British Columbia, actually," said the fellow. "But I used to know Earl in the old days. Thought I'd look him up. We go back a lotta years. Some of our mutual acquaintances down at the King Eddie, hm, they told me I should try here."

"He has a house near there, you know."

"Yessir, we go back a lotta years."

"I can get you his address if you'd like."

"Oh, no, Ma'am. You see, I already tried his house. It's still locked up. Boarded up. Looks like no one's been there for quite a stretch."

"Well, isn't that the strangest thing," said Mrs. Miller.

It wasn't strange in the slightest. It only proved her suspicions: that old fool was shacked up with Julie Belanger.

"You say you knew Mr. Claney here?"

"Long time ago."

"I don't suppose you're thinking about moving back to Saskatoon, are you?"

"No'm. Not likely. Everyone's gone. Wouldn't know a soul."

"Well, you know, I might just be able to help you. Find Earl, that is. He has a friend, her name is Julie Belanger. He might just be staying with her till he gets back on his feet."

"Got an address?"

"Well, Mr. ah, I could phone over for you. I have the number somewhere in…"

"Oh, no. Don't phone. I'd love to surprise him. The old duffer. Love to surprise him."

Mrs. Miller had darted into the kitchen. She found the file card with Julie's address and phone number on it and removed it from her bulletin board. She could hear her new girl downstairs vacuuming.

"It wouldn't be any trouble," she muttered, padding towards the telephone.

He was suddenly right there, hulking in front of her. He had moved with the speed of a great animal. He plucked the file card from her hand.

"Guess you didn't hear me," he said with a toothy smile. "I said I'd like to surprise him."

Mrs. Miller's heart was pattering away like a snare drum. There was no need to be frightened, no immediate danger. But she stepped back in alarm and right then, perhaps, he might have seen the fear in her eyes.

"Sit down," he said. "Over there."

She sat down on the sofa.

"You know, some folks just don't listen. Gosh, you tell em real nice an quiet, they don't even hear ya. Tell em louder, they still don't hear ya. You yell at them, they think you're a *violent individual*. Tell me, ma'am, does the expression violent individual mean something to you? Do I strike you as a violent individual?"

Mrs. Miller tried to say something, but her voice was gone.

"Bet you didn't even hear me. Were you listenin to what I said?"

"Yes!" she cried.

"Then answer my question."

"Oh, yes!" she cried once again. "I heard every word."

"Then answer my goddam question."

"Excuse me, mister, what was the question again?"

"That's just what I was talkin about. I try my damndest to make myself understood, and women are the worst, they are by far the worst, they just don't listen. Hell, I could be dying here, I could be gaspin out my last dyin wishes, and you'd just walk right over me, and that. makes. me. see. red. I could be Jesus Christ hisself, come to heal the infirm, bleedin from the scalp with the hounds a hell at his feet beggin for a glass a water an *Whats at y'say? What did you say yer name was? Jesus who?* Well, lady, you got me real mad. You got me clean off on the wrong goddam track, you got me wonderin what the hell I'm here for."

"I was only trying to be helpful."

The old fellow stood up suddenly. "Where's the can at?"

"Wha...wha?"

"The *can*! You got a *can*, dontcha?"

"Oh, that way. Second door on the left."

He stomped out of the living room and down the hall, roaring profanities all the way, and it seemed as though he were talking to himself. She prayed the new girl would keep on vacuuming and not come up the stairs or it might set him off again. The man began to urinate, but it didn't sound like the doings of an old man. It sounded like a big old horse, and it almost drowned out the sound of his raging voice.

JULIE

Saskatoon, mid–April 2003

"No, Sammy, you gotta bet first. You like that card? Hey? You wanna see me, raise me?"

"I can see you fine," Sammy said.

"I mean, Sammy, do you wanna bet on your card."

Sammy threw in another button.

"You like that card enough, Sammy, you can raise me."

"Raise you?"

"Up the bet some."

"They're just buttons."

"I know they're just buttons, Sammy, but pretend they're real money. You wanna win all you can, see?"

"No, thank you," Sammy said. "I'm stayin put."

"Well, podner, here's what I got. Whada you got?"

The phone rang. Earl could hear Julie's voice in the living room. "Yeah?" she said, and the volume on the tv set came down a notch or two. "Speak up," she said. "Who is this?"

"Lemme see those cards," said Earl.

Sammy put his cards down one by one, and he smiled and jiggled his shoulders.

"You got a full house, Sammy. Did you know you had a full house?"

"Do I know you?" asked Julie in the kitchen.

"Why do they call it a full house? There's no house."

"Who's that?" Earl shouted. "What does he want?"

"Speak up," said Julie. "A bad man where? Speak up, lady. You work for who?"

There was only silence from the living room, followed by the sound of Julie replacing the phone.

"Oh, hell," she said to no one.

"Who was that?" croaked Earl, as Julie came into the kitchen.

"I couldn't tell," said Julie. "She kept whisperin as though the guy might hear her."

"What guy?"

"She wouldn't say his name, she sounded kinda mousey. I could hardly hear."

"Hey, Earl?" said Sammy. "Why do they call it a full house?"

"Wasn't askin for me was he?"

Suddenly the expression on Julie's face seemed to stiffen, and she marched around Earl to where Sammy was sitting.

"Up you go," she said to Sammy. "Quiet as you can be. And don't come down until I tell you. Got that?"

"We were just playin—"

"Get," cried Julie, and Sammy slouched out of the room.

"What's goin on here?" said Earl.

"I think I figgered it out. I think it might be Mervy. Someone's tryin to warn me. That was one a his floozies. I think he's on his way over here an he's probably drunk."

"Well, I'll be damned. Call the cops."

"Never does no good."

"Call the cops, Julie."

"No. No. I haven't seen that son of a bitch for four years. Earl, you gotta answer the door. Tell him we don't live here no more. If he starts comin upstairs, yell real loud. Say, *I told ya, she don't live here no more. You got that?*"

"What about you?"

"I don't know, I might be wrong. This is just in case. Just do it. Set down there with the tv on. Go, Earl."

Earl padded out into the living room. Perhaps it was better not to phone the cops. They might end up asking him some questions. He stood alone, scratched his elbows, looked around for a weapon of any kind. A stool. A chair. No, no damn good. An old board? His gaze fell on a fire extinguisher resting in the corner of the front hall. He bent down, gasping, wincing, and picked up the device. It consisted of a large red cylinder with a two-handled pump mechanism on the top. *Dry Chemical multi-purpose type, UL Rated.* The question was, did you spray the guy in the face or did you throw the thing and brain him? Maybe first you sprayed him, then you brained him.

Earl placed the fire extinguisher on the sofa and covered it up with a wool blanket. He hadn't gone toe-to-toe with a real scrapper in a long time, except once when he was drunk at the racetrack, and that didn't hardly count. This time he'd have to play it sly and smart, catch his opponent off guard.

Earl was beginning to puff and wheeze. *Don't go havin no episode*, he told himself. *Wrong time for a goddam episode.* He took his place on the sofa next to the fire extinguisher. He heard some scuffling and whispering back and forth upstairs. That would be Julie tending to the boy. He waited until things got quiet up there. Julie would be laying low somewheres. Under the bed maybe. Standing at the back of her closet behind her clothes.

He lifted the comforter and peered at the fire extinguisher. He cradled it in his arms.

To Operate:
- *Hold upright*
- *Aim nozzle at base of fire*
- *Squeeze handles*
- *Use side-to-side motion*
- *Range: 10 to 15 feet*

For wood, paper, cloth, plastic, rubber, flammable liquids, grease, gas and electrical fires.

"Don't say nothin about oil rig workers or mean drunks," said Earl, and pointed the channel changer at the television set. He pressed POWER and Julie's program returned, and just then someone was knocking on the front door.

"Jesus Christ," said Earl. He replaced the blanket over the fire extinguisher and staggered to his feet.

The knock came again, more of a thump than a knock.

"Here goes," said Earl, and opened the door.

An old fellow in a black coat with wooden pegs for buttons stood before him. Mervy Carlin was older than Earl had expected.

"Yessir," he said. "What can I do ya for?"

The big fellow just stood there. He said, "Do you know who I am?"

Earl squinted at the man's face, but he was standing back from the main focus of the light in the front hall.

"No," he said. No way could he slam the door in the guy's face. He'd have to con him real good.

"Come in, come in," said Earl.

The old fellow came in and closed the doors. He wasn't holding a gun, and he didn't seem to be drunk. Earl would have smelled it on him. He just stood there, a tall old fellow, stooped and sleepy-eyed.

"You got the slightest idea who I am?"

"Should I?" said Earl, heading for the sofa.

"If your name is Earl Claney, you should."

Earl felt a thumping in his heart. He turned to face the man.

"Siddown," he said to the big fellow. "Siddown."

Earl sat down himself but the big fellow remained standing. He thought he recognized him now, but wasn't that man supposed to be dead? That's what that investigator fellow had said. But Earl thought he recognized this man from the trial. In spite of the fifty years gone by. At the trial he had been more subdued, leaner, but yes, Earl recognized him. The grinding and clicking he did with his back teeth, that nervous tic.

"This don't have to take very long," the man said. "I think you know why I'm here."

"I will if ya tell me."

"My name is Cletis Bulger."

"Oh?"

"Don't play dumb with me, Mr. Claney. Do I have to spell it out for ya?"

"Fraid so."

"You do some drinkin at an establishment known as the King Eddie. Do a lot of talkin there, dontcha."

"If you say I do, then I guess I do."

"Did some talkin about hidin them tips? All that money your brother stole? Buried somewheres, wouldn't dig it up. All that silver?"

"I dunno what in the hell you're—"

"Shutup."

The man reached into his pocket and produced a rectangular disc of some kind. He held it under the light by the sofa so that Earl could see it. He squinted at the object, a coin enclosed in plastic.

"This here's a King Edward fifty-cent piece." He put the coin back in his pocket. "A sailor of my acquaintance offered me a thousand dollars for the coin, no questions asked. You must be wonderin where I got this coin, Mr. Claney."

"No, I wasn't wonderin at all."

"Another old acquaintance of mine, I relieved him of this coin because, see, he wouldn't be needin it any more. If I said the name Bishop Montgomery, would that name mean something to you, sir?"

"That fella got kilt on the Coast?"

"That would be him," said Bulger. "We took a little trip to Saskatoon in my taxi a long time ago. Made the acquaintance of your brother. I believe Joe was his name?"

"You goddam know it was."

"My good friend Mr. Montgomery seemed awful darn eager to get his money back. He said some of the coins had sentimental value for his father. Sentimental value, Mr. Claney."

"So?"

"They was just silver dollars. How could you be sentimental about a bunch of silver dollars? All they cost back then was a dollar. Well, as you can see, I didn't sell this here fifty-cent piece to my friend the sailor for a thousand dollars. I looked it up, see? It's worth at least ten times that. And I got to thinkin, maybe that's what made Bishy— we all called him Bishy—that's what made Bishy's father so goshdarn sentimental about them coins away back in 1951. They was collector coins, scarce as chicken's teeth."

The man's eyes lost their focus, his voice went dreamy, as though he were talking to himself. "I couldn't confirm this absolutely," he continued. "About the coins. I tried getting in touch with a German fellow of my acquaintance. Way back in the Banff days. Find out what was really in that golf bag. Drove out there back in March, but I guess he wasn't home. When you really want help, I guess no one's ever home."

"Did you break inta my house?" said Earl, trying to get his breath, trying to play for time.

"Why, yes, I took a little trip out here when you were indisposed over at that nosey woman's place. Mrs. Miller's little home for old farts. Couldn't find a thing at your house, but I did find out where you liked to raise a glass, Mr. Claney. Met some fine old boys at the King Eddie. Imagine, sir, the King Edward! Don't that seem ironical? Well, sir, I put two and two together, and I'd be willin to bet your brother tossed that golf bag into the river to make us think all the money was in it. What do you think of my theory?"

"It's probly bullshit. How the hell should I know?"

Earl's hands began to move under the blanket. He prayed they would not begin to shake.

"What if them coins was worth a pile, Bulger? Say fifty thou? Why not just rob a bank and get more money? Wouldn't that be a lot simpler and less trouble?"

"Well, sir, I done time for that money. I done time for it, because…"

The old man's face was turning red, he leaned forward and stooped down to glare at Earl nose to nose. He swallowed and began to shake his head and roar like a deranged bull.

"Because I got betrayed!"

"Quiet down, fella. Don't get so excited. You'd think it was *me* who betrayed you."

"You told the judge I planned to kill your brother! You stood there and told a baldfaced lie! I didn't plan nothin, I just got a bit excited, see? Do you see, Mr. Claney? A man gets excited now an then!"

Bulger turned about abruptly, strode towards the front door, plucked Julie's porcelain tiger off the stand, and tossed it from one big hand to the other like it was a football.

"Where's it at?"

Earl said nothing.

Suddenly Bulger lobbed the porcelain tiger right at Earl's head. Earl ducked sideways and the flying tiger sailed past his ear and shattered on the wall behind him. Bulger shuffled over to Julie's television set, snapped it off, heaved it up into his arms, yanking out the plug, and swung it over his head.

"Wait!" cried Earl.

He was gathering the comforter from the sofa, inch by inch. Slowly Bulger brought down the television set and held it to his chest as Earl pulled the entire comforter, bunched up, into his shivering arms. He was going for the look of an invalid preparing for death. And then he tossed the comforter at Bulger, who found it suddenly draped over his head while he was embracing Julie's tv set. Like a magus lost in the bounty of his own robes, Bulger stood there a moment too long.

"You ain't seen my Sunday punch," gasped Earl.

He was holding the fire extinguisher in both hands. With all his strength he heaved the metal cylinder, it caught Bulger somewhere low on his shrouded face and he fell backwards into the front hall, clutching the set in his arms. Bulger tripped on the comforter and went down. The fire extinguisher clattered to the floor, and the television set lay miraculously unharmed on his chest. Earl glared down at the big man.

"You say I got somethin you want, fella? You kill my brother in the prime of his life and *I owe you* somethin? Either you got a screw loose or a real bad memry."

Bulger lay still, breathing noisily. He shoved the television set off his chest, rolled over, groaned.

Earl looked around for something else to throw. There were knives in the kitchen but he didn't want that. He wanted something heavy. At last he spotted a large unopened can of paint. He had no idea why Julie might have left it in the living room, but it might just do the job. He picked up the can and held it in both hands.

Bulger was on his feet, swaying, rubbing his jaw. It was hard for a short man to brain a taller one, the angles were all wrong, you had to aim upstairs.

"You get the hell outa here," said Earl.

"Why?" said Bulger. "Is your brother gonna come back?"

"What?"

Bulger lurched forward, wheezing.

"I said, sir, is your brother Joseph plannin to come back from the dead and wreak a vengeance on me? You goin to sick his immortal ghost on me?"

The paint can seemed to fly of its own accord from Earl's hands straight for Bulger's head. Bulger lurched to his left and the paint can struck him on the elbow and crashed to the floor. Bulger staggered forward, shaking the pain from his arm.

"Because I don't see no such Joseph, sir," he gasped. "All I see is a wore-out little bastard at the end of his rope, who's gonna tell me where my rightful money is at."

He rushed at Claney and grabbed him by the neck with both hands, as though Claney were an old rooster ready for the chopping block. Back and forth he shook him until Earl could scarcely see, and Bulger broke out into rainbows of shining light like a great avenging bird ripping meat from carrion, and dropped him at last on the floor.

"Just desserts. When I say just desserts, does that mean something to you, Mr. Claney? Because I come here to collect on my just desserts, see? I got something comin to me, Mr. Claney. I got my claims. Does justice mean anything to you, Mr. Claney? I think that I can say that I know something about justice. Am I bein clear to you, sir?"

Claney strained in his gullet to tell the fellow to fuck himself.

"Where is it, you little fool? Where is the money?"

Not here, Earl tried to say, but he couldn't speak.

Not here, someone else said.

"You can't shoot that thing," Bulger gasped. "Now. just. put. it. down."

Earl opened his eyes and the rainbow lights were still pulsing and Bulger was a monstrous neon sign in the flapping shape of a vulture and Julie was a smaller neon sign in the shape of a woman.

"That thing would knock you clean back into yesterday."

"Get."

"That old thing won't even shoot and you know it. I've known bitches tougher than you, sweetheart, and they all end up in the same position. Begging."

"Get out."

"You're gonna make me?"

Silence.

"I said, sweetheart, are going to—"

The blast came like a concussion to the entire room: it detonated Earl awake, blasted the neon out of Bulger as he seemed to march backwards, as though in stomping backwards he would catch up to the bone gristle blood and flesh that flew from his left arm and shoulder, useless now, dangling like a chain, and Julie driven in the opposite direction, hard against the wall and sliding to the floor.

Shotgun by her side, she remained upright, transfixed by what she had done, glancing briefly at Earl down on the floor, then gawking at the great writhing carcass on the edge of her living room rug, the venomous thing that Cletis Bulger was still trying to be.

Earl woke up in a hospital bed feeling strangely rested. He had a sore throat, and two fingers of his right hand had gone purple and were bound in aluminum splints. Julie was looking down on him, clutching her jacket to her body with one hand.

"Where's the boy?" Earl rasped.

"He's okay. He had a bad scare and the doctor give him somethin."

"You all right?"

"I got a bruise right here," she said, pointing to the bicep on her right arm. "You wouldn't believe the size of it."

"The old fella?"

"Bulger, he's in bad shape. I guess the police was lookin for him. Guy from the cops, he's comin back up here to talk to you in a minute. He knows about Bulger."

Earl nodded.

"But you knew he was out there, didn't you Earl. This Bulger fellow. You knew quite a few things I didn't."

Earl shook his head almost imperceptively. "They told me the bastard was dead."

"What was he lookin for? Earl?"

He looked up at her.

"Earl, you think you got a choice here? You think you can come into my home as my guest and bring that hellhound with you, and the kid upstairs, and mum's the word? Well, think again, you old coot. You got some—"

"Money."

"What?"

"Money got buried a long time ago. More than fifty years ago. As far as I know, it's still in the ground."

"A lotta money, you mean?"

Earl shrugged.

"Earl?"

"It's a bunch of old money, old coins and silver dollars and such. Might be worth a few thou, maybe more."

"Fifty years ago?" said Julie. She was whispering. She shot a furtive glance over her shoulder. "You mean you never dug it up? You never spent it? Just let it set there?"

"My brother stole it."

"So?"

"My brother died for that money. I didn't want nothin to do with it. I couldn't bear to go near it. Gave me the creeps just to think about it. Bad luck money, that's what it is."

Julie sat down in a chair by Earl's bed. He could just barely glimpse her from the corner of his eyes. He could have turned his head to face her but his neck and throat were too sore to move. He wished that he could just hold her hand and lie there in complete silence.

A large, stormy looking man entered the room. Earl could tell at a glance that the man was a cop. The man turned to Julie, his eyes glowering below a pair of bushy eyebrows.

"I think you might wanta know," he said to her. "Our Mr. Bulger didn't make it."

"Well, thank the Christ," Earl said, and closed his eyes.

PART V: SILVER

A FRIENDLY CONVERSATION

"We're not having an affair," said Shmata. "It's not like that. We're just seeing each other. Now and then."

"Then what have I been doin?"

"I don't know," said Shmata. "Enjoying her company?"

His friend shrugged. Bork's pub was adrift with cigarette smoke and Letourneau's despondency.

"What does Francie say about all of this?"

"There's nothin to say," said Letourneau, a little too loud. "Nothin happened. Except…"

"Except what?" said Shmata.

"Haw. Now I got your attention."

They had chosen Bork's to have a talk about Shmata's future with the Service, but somehow they had gotten side-tracked. Perhaps Letourneau felt the need to confess his sins.

"You were about to tell me something," said Shmata.

"Nothin happened between me and Bertha."

"Except?"

"Except, Shmata, I got the stupids. I got off my game. I made mistakes, goddam it, don't you see?"

What he saw was that Letourneau had acquired a schoolboy crush on Bertha, and that was painful for him to admit. And Letourneau had dropped the ball on the Montgomery/Spencer case, and that was painful to admit. And he had sicced the Vancouver boys on Cletis Bulger only to find out that Bulger was in his own back yard, and that was hard to admit. And Shmata and Bertha, in various ways, had saved his ass before anyone at the Service had found out. And no doubt that was tough to admit. These things all seemed to point in one direction: the indomitable Letourneau was suffering from burnout.

Shmata steered the conversation, as carefully as he could, to the subject of Letourneau's long-suffering wife.

"What the fuck am I gonna do, Shmata?"

"Phone her up. Take her out to dinner. Give her the time of her life. Take the mothballs off your wallet and live a little."

Letourneau's eyes narrowed, and the bushy eyebrows were massing for a storm.

"I can't believe I'm hearin this from you. I'm a married man, Shmata. She's all yours."

"I meant Francie, not Bertha."

"Francie? What's she got to do with all this?"

"You mean none of this has affected her?"

"Like what?"

"I don't know," said Shmata. "Late hours? Neglect? Bad things you bring home from work?"

"Mind your own fuckin business, Shmata. You take her out."

"Take who out?"

"Now look who's got the stupids," bellowed Letourneau triumphantly, with perhaps a touch of humour.

"Well, Mike, you've had what might be described as an off month or two, but I still envy you."

"You really do have the stupids, Shmata. What's to envy?"

"You're married to a good woman. You've got a family, a good job. You've risen high in the Service. Your days and nights must be pretty full."

Letourneau grunted something Shmata couldn't hear.

"Shmata, if you had a chance to be married again, would you take it?"

Shmata shook his head and then shrugged.

"There's a straight answer if ever I heard one." Letourneau lit up another smoke and gazed off at the assembled crowd at Bork's.

"You know what gripes me?" demanded Letourneau.

"Are we still talking about the sad mysteries of love?"

"I sure as fuck hope not, Shmata. I'm thinkin about Julie Belanger and her ten gauge. What gripes me is that none of us could run Bulger down. I mean he was in his late seventies for godsake. And this slip of a woman, with one pull of the trigger. Bang."

"Bang indeed."

"You know the shotgun wasn't registered?"

Shmata had heard this, but he didn't want Letourneau to know that he'd been snooping around for information.

"Is she going to be charged?"

"No way we're chargin her," Letourneau went on. "She'll have to pay a fine and she loses the gun, but no criminal charges. She's a goddam hero."

He looked up at Shmata and touched his temple with a large index finger. "Say, did you know that our boys found a coin in the pocket of our friend, the late Mr. Bulger? Yep. A collector coin in a plastic slab. You taught me that word."

"What kind of a coin?"

"Half dollar. We thought maybe he'd found the missin coins in Earl Clany's digs, but according to Earl, he stole it off Bishop Montgomery when he beat him to death."

Shmata was all attention. "You mean that Montgomery had valuable coins on his person when—"

"If Claney was telling the truth. For a moment last week, before I talked with Claney again, I thought maybe we were onto the mother lode."

"You actually believe that golf bag is going to show up?"

"Well, Bill, between you an me, old Bulger said a few things before they took him into surgery. He thought maybe old Earl had them stashed away."

"Or Montgomery had them all along."

"You mean they never got stolen in the first place?" said Letourneau. "And Montgomery only claimed they were?"

"I don't know," said Shmata. "Do you believe Bulger?"

"I don't know what to believe," said Letourneau. "If we found the golf bag I wouldn't even know what to do with the coins." Letourneau was rotating the burning ash on the end of his cigarette in the groove of the ashtray. He looked up. "Almost forgot, Shmata. We came here to talk about you."

"Yes, I suppose so."

"I don't know what to say."

"Letourneau, the chief still hasn't returned my call. Just tell me that you've brought it up with him."

"Of course I brought it up with the chief. I told him you wanted to come back part-time, and you know him. He nods his head and he thinks, and he thinks some more. A day or so later he says to me *What the hell does that mean,* like he's never heard the phrase part-time before. So I tell him again, you want to do a reduced work load with Major Crimes till you're sixty-five."

"And?"

"No way in hell."

"What do you mean? Letourneau?"

"He says he's surprised you'd even consider it. No way the chief is gonna spend that kind of money on a halftime guy when he can hire a new guy fulltime at the same salary."

"I already told you, Letourneau, I could take a cut in salary. I wouldn't have to go in at the top of my range."

"Nope."

"Why not?"

"You've already retired, Shmata. Besides, the union wouldn't go for it. They would insist you get hired at your old level."

"But surely, Letourneau, if I *stipulated*—"

Letourneau was shaking his head.

"Is this what the chief said, or is this what Mike Letourneau says?"

"It's what everyone says. I thought this was just a friendly conversation, Shmata. Not a fuckin job interview."

"This isn't a job interview, this is one friend telling another one he's just shut the door."

"Shmata, cool down. I'm just sayin."

"You've got some real whack up there, Mike. You could talk some sense into these guys if you had a mind to."

"Maybe I could if I was still on the job."

"What?"

"As of this week...I'm on a little extended vacation."

"What?"

"The chief says I'm...you know..."

"No, I don't know. Tell me."

"I told him to fuck himself."

"You told him to...on my behalf?"

"No," Letourneau growled. "I just told him to fuck himself. It was just one of those spur of the moment things."

They stayed together at the bar long enough for Shmata to get one of his old sad yearnings for a whiskey and a beer chaser. They tried to commiserate. They tried to talk. Finally, Shmata stood up to go. He tossed a bill onto the table and waved to his old friend. The wave meant, I will get home on my own.

"I'll see you around," said Letourneau, without conviction, still seated at the table, once more rotating his cigarette in the groove of the ashtray.

BERTHA OF THE SORROWS

Saskatoon, mid-May 2003

Bertha Eeling was faced with a new challenge: how to nudge Bill Shmata away from his present state of celibacy and into her bed. Surely that was where they were headed. They had progressed from lunches to suppers at the Chow Mein Palace to walks down by the river. The longer they talked into the evenings, the longer they walked. She began to notice the compact solidity of his body, the strength in his stride, the way his face lit up when she arrived at their secret meeting places.

Bill Shmata was twelve years older than she. Bertha had always had a weakness for older men, an easily controlled one, the sort of weakness that never lapsed into silliness. Until recently, however, she had thought of this weakness as a strength, or at least as a safe zone. Early on in her twenties, she had found herself avoiding the young eager ones. But now that she thought about it, she had to admit that there were advantages to going with a man who didn't mind initiating some action. Bill Shmata was not much in the initiation department. Lately he'd been moody. It was something to do with Letourneau, she was pretty sure, but Bill was too held-in to unburden himself about it.

One of their favourite walking places was above the river on the east side of town and through the university campus. They could take in a film at the student theatre and see no one they knew. They could walk past the music department tower and hear the most exquisite sounds come piping out all in a jumble from the open windows of the practice rooms. They could take a path right down to the river and watch the nesting birds, the gulls, geese and pelicans go through their domestic routines.

Bertha and Shmata had begun to hold hands, and surely that meant something.

One bright evening in the middle of May, strolling between two tyndallstone residences on the campus, they had both gone silent. They walked across the quad listening to the trills of songbirds, and then they took the Meewasin Trail north above the river. They were headed for the CPR bridge when Shmata broke the silence.

"Earl Claney had another seizure this morning."

"Oh no."

"The boy was with him when he had it. Julie Belanger's boy, Sammy."

"Yes?"

"I guess they're both pretty worried," he said.

The great wooden bridge loomed ahead of them as they walked. A pair of cyclists hummed past them. Other walkers were out enjoying the evening. A pair of birders stood in the middle of the old bridge, scanning the river below with their binoculars.

"I guess Earl and Sammy have grown pretty close over the past month or so," said Bill.

Earl Claney's imminent death. That would be another sad chapter to her Bulger/Claney file. With each new revelation, the file kept growing larger. The Claney case was beginning to make most of her other annals look dull and terse by comparison.

"That sister of Claney's," said Bertha, "has she started to hover?"

"She's in town right now."

"I wonder if Earl has included Julie in his will."

"From what I hear from Frenchie Demain," said Shmata, "Claney is a procrastinator. Frenchie goes to visit him. And Earl has been too weak to get up and get his affairs in order. I wouldn't be surprised if Julie doesn't get a cent."

"Oh, God, this is so sad. She'll have to try and find another job washing old ladies."

"Guess so," Bill muttered.

"Julie has no job, and she has to pay rent for that house. And she and her son will lose their friend."

Bill was looking at her.

"Are those tears?" he said. "You haven't even met them."

"Claney and the boy," she sobbed. "They were both paper boys!"

Bill took her into his arms and they stayed that way, swaying by the side of the trail as cyclists sped past.

"You'd think the old fart would have told the boy by now where the coins were buried," she said.

"You'd think so," said Bill. "Claney thought they were bad luck. That's all he's ever said about them."

Bertha was blowing her nose and Bill stood by solicitously.

"Do I look a mess?"

"You look fine."

"What if they dredged for the coins or found them in the house or some place? Who would own them legally?"

"I'm not sure," said Bill, "but there's been a lot of publicity surrounding Bulger's death. If Julie found the coins tomorrow, and word got out, she might get a phonecall from a lawyer for Montgomery's daughter in Vancouver. But I doubt it. I'm not even sure the coins went into the river, the really valuable ones."

"So if they *did* exist, and they were found, whoever found them would have to sell them on the Q.T.? The black market or something?"

Bill nodded. He seemed lost in thought.

"I doubt if there'd be a problem. After all these years, who could prove they belonged to anyone?"

They resumed walking and ventured out onto the old bridge. It was a high wooden trestle built for the trains to cross the river, and it had a wooden walkway with two-by-four rails for pedestrian traffic. It creaked in places as the river flowed below them, almost a hundred feet down. Bertha walked gingerly and Bill had to urge her along to the halfway point.

"Of course, there's another way of thinking about the Montgomery estate," said Bill, waiting for Bertha to catch up. "If the coins were ever found, even if Montgomery's daughter heard about them, she would not try to recover them."

"Insurance, you mean? They've already collected?"

"Oh, I suppose that's possible. But think of the publicity. People will talk. People will want to read your own account. Reporters flock to a story like that. Two respectable bluebloods get a friend to do their dirty work and Joseph Claney dies as a result. Think of the black mark on the two families."

"Time to lay the whole thing to rest," said Bertha.

She was thinking once again about her Claney/Bulger file. Every week or two there was a new angle to explore or a new development on the case that prompted her to hurry down to her office and add it to her account. More than once she had written a tentative conclusion to the case only to find out that the story had not quite ended.

Bill was pointing down at the base of the trestle.

"There's where Joseph Claney hit the water."

She ventured to peek over the side of the railings. The heights were getting to her.

"First the golf bag," said Bill, "then Joe Claney. I had to go over to Julie's to tidy up some loose ends for my records. I keep notes. Little Sammy was there, and he claims the golf bag was filled with junk. Julie said Sammy should learn to keep his mouth shut."

"Full of junk?" said Bertha. "The golf bag?"

Almost apologetically Bill said, "I keep wondering where Earl would go to hide the coins. If they existed. And how much he really told the boy."

"Perhaps they did exist," said Bertha, "and he just got rid of them."

"Sammy doesn't think so."

"So you went over there to get your records straight? And not to talk about Claney's bloody coins? Bill, tell me you haven't been talking to the boy about Claney's bloody coins."

"Bloody coins indeed."

"William Shmata," she said. "Were you in your treasure hunting mode?"

"No, I was just asking Sammy what he remembered about the night Bulger came to call."

"Letourneau still has you digging things up for him?"

"No," said Shmata. "Letourneau's still on vacation and we aren't...I just can't quit wondering."

Bertha said, "Neither can I."

She looked down at the water as it swirled between the girders of the trestle and flowed around the deep channels and gravel bars north of the bridge.

"And Earl's big brother was only twenty years old," she said, and her tears returned.

"Do you want to go back?" said Bill, and took her hand.

"Don't you see?" she said.

"Yes, yes."

"It's all so sad."

"Yes," he said.

They walked back to their cars near the university residences and stood beneath a large budding elm. The light in the northwest was fading and the campus was enveloped in darkness and fragrance from the lilacs and early flowers. Bill put his arms around Bertha in what seemed to be an attempt to comfort her, but somewhere along the way, he began to kiss her ear, her face and then her neck, and she began to kiss back, and soon they were caught up in something else entirely, moaning like campus lovers, and Bertha mumbled something about going back to his place because hers was a mess, and yes, he said, and yes she said, and yes, they climbed into separate cars and sped across the river to Shmata's townhouse.

Perhaps, like Letourneau, Bertha was having a midlife crisis. She thought of her lovemaking with Shmata as a form of consolation for her sadness. She now saw sadness wherever she went among the files of the Police Service; wherever she went in the city—as though the sadness had been waiting for her all these years, waiting to envelope her. She could scarcely think about the current financial plight of Julie Belanger without sinking into misery. She had never in her life been like this, a damp-eyed bleeding heart moving around the city to participate in a great bottomless feast of pity. She wasn't in a deep depression, nothing like that. Her weeping spells never lasted long, she was down one day and up the next, but she worried that one of these bouts might break out when she was least expecting it. At a work session with Letourneau, or shopping at the downtown mall.

But now she had this other thing in her life. A new man in her life. A great walker and listener with a nice compact, consoling body with curly black and silver hair on his chest. A source of frequent joy and hope. She wondered if they all somehow went together, this reticent lover and these joys and sorrows.

One night, alone in her house, she sought consolation in another source. She hadn't done this in a long time, but now the sadness was on her again, and the urge was irresistible. She descended the stairs to her basement and pulled down an old suitcase, dusted it off and hauled it upstairs. She opened the suitcase and poked around among the keepsakes of her grandfather. At last she came upon his journal. He had kept it for a few years in order to continue the work his wife had begun, and then he had stopped. She lifted out the notebook. She would eventually take it down to the archives so that it could join the pile of note-books kept by the grandmother Bertha had never known. She would do this soon, so that the notebooks could lie together. But in spite of the almost obsessive dullness of her grandfather's jottings, in spite of the fact that her grandmother was by far the superior raconteur, she had never wanted to let go of this last notebook. Not because it had hidden depths of richness or even much of a nostalgic value, but because it was *his*. In his voice. The man who had raised her after the accident that took her parents.

She brought it over to the kitchen table and brewed a small pot of tea, then took the tea, some biscuits and the journal to bed with her.

His earliest entries, as she well knew, were all about birds and weather. *March 17. Geese back on river. Three mating pairs and a lone goose.*

Once more, as she sipped her tea in bed, the tears threatened to flow. An old man who has lost his family, his wife, who is now saddled with a little girl to raise: he comes down to the river and sees a goose without a mate. It was all so sad. As sad as the prospect of Claney's death and the plight of Julie Belanger and her son.

But why go on like this when Julie and her boy were alive and healthy for godsake? And instead of getting charged for manslaughter, Julie Belanger had become a folk hero in her own neighbourhood. Reporters had been showing up at her door.

Nevertheless Bertha wept, and then returned to her notebooks. *June 4, wheeled Berta out to see the motor boats on the river. A noisy lot. Cut her hair with kitchen scissors. A first for me!*

Berta! she sighed and wiped her eyes. He had always called her Berta. How sad. She wanted to call Bill. It was midnight, and he would be asleep, but she really had to talk to someone. She rang his number. He sounded drugged.

"I had to phone someone," she said. "I guess you're it."

"Should I come over?"

"No, I just need to talk."

"Okay," he said with a yawn.

"I think I know what's going on here," said Bertha. "I'm not really grieving for the Claneys or Julie and little Sammy."

"You're not."

"No, Bill, I'm really grieving for myself. I mean, not just myself, but for my whole family. My grandad who had to raise me after he lost his wife to T.B. My parents who died in that horrible accident. My grandmother that I never met. That's what this is all about."

"Well, I could come over, Bertha."

"My Grandad called me Berta," she said tearfully. "I've been reading his journals. The ones he began when Granny died. I think he must have been trying to keep her voice alive by writing these weekly entries."

"Are you feeling any better now?"

"I suppose so," she said. "It's all a matter of coming to terms with your true feelings, isn't it."

She heard him groan at the other end. William Shmata was not big on coming to terms with one's true feelings. She promised not to phone him again in the middle of the night, hung up, and returned to her grandfather's journal. She was beginning to nod.

What if Bill began to call her Berta? How would she feel about that?

August 19, went to see crows flocking up by the San at sunset. Great lot of them, more than last yr at this time. Strange thing happened. A person, young lad perhaps, scurrying about on the grounds of the San. One second he's there, the next he's gone. Poof.

"Now what are you on about, Grandad?" she said out loud, yawning. She had read all these entries before, but she had forgotten about this one.

Aug 20-21, Miss Moritz has taken over for the time being. Berta gets along very nicely with her. She likes to curl B's hair, says we need a dog.

"Ah, yes," Bertha sighed. "Good old Miss Moritz."

She couldn't really remember the woman, she was too young, but she had a picture somewhere of Miss Moritz sitting on the front stoop of their house.

Aug 23, went back to the San. Took a little wander over the grounds where our young adventurer had been traipsing about in the dark. Found several air vents. He disappeared, all right. Down an air vent! Mystery solved, my dear.

"My dear?" Bertha whispered. "Of course."

She too had solved a little mystery. Her grandfather wasn't trying to keep his dead wife's voice alive; he must have been addressing his entries directly to her. As though she were still alive. It might have kept him going through all his loneliness and grief, to be able to address her like that. *My dear.* It would have been right around the time poor Earl Claney lost his brother.

Bertha laid her journal on the floor and turned out her bedside lamp, intent on sleep. How many times had she read those passages before, but not until now had it occurred to her what exactly her grandfather had been up to. No matter. Sleep, that was the answer to all questions.

Just as sleep seemed to be drifting in at last, Bertha's eyes flew open. She sat up in bed, turned on her light. She fumbled for her reading glasses and picked up her grandfather's journal. She checked the exact dates of the entries she had just read.

"Oh, good Lord."

She had promised not to phone him again, but this was important. She dialled his number.

"Yes?" said Bill, and this time he didn't sound drugged. He sounded wide awake.

"Bill," she said. "You are not going to believe this."

"Believe what?"

"Don't get your hopes up. I might be barking up the wrong tree."

"Bertha, what are you talking about?"

"Bill, I think you'd better come over here."

OCEAN RECONNAISANCE

Saskatoon, late May 2003

Bertha and Shmata had just concluded their first lovers' quarrel. Perhaps "suspended" would be a better word, because this quarrel had some potential for further engagements. It concerned the role of young Sammy in their reconnaissance mission at the old San. Should he be allowed to come and participate?

Shmata thought yes and Bertha said no. It was too dangerous, she said. His mother would never let him go, she said. It would not be dangerous at all, Shmata countered. He had explored root cellars before, and he had never heard of a cave-in. Not in Saskatoon. The soil was too stable for cave-ins. Bertha said nonsense, there was alkali in the soil. It was unstable, and what about that terrible cave-in where the two young people were killed? That was in Medicine Hat. But wasn't the soil considered even stabler in Medicine Hat? No, it's not. Yes, it is. They quarry the soil around Medicine Hat for potter's clay, for godsake. Potter's clay? Shmata was stumped on that one.

It was Bertha's firm opinion that the boy should stay up on top as a lookout. No, Shmata countered, he should be allowed the thrill of the search. It was something he'd remember for the rest of his life. He couldn't remember the thrill of the search, Bertha argued, if he was dead at the bottom of a cave-in. If the passages under the grounds of the San had not caved in by now, Shmata claimed, there was little likelihood of them caving in just on the day of their trip down there. Besides, he added, they would need someone who could explore nooks and crannies.

Bertha was appalled. Shmata would send a nine year-old boy into a dark cave because he was the right size? No, Shmata countered, they would be careful.

The argument took a different course at this point and turned into a debate on male versus female common sense. It was typical of men, Bertha argued, to assume that a dangerous mission was worth any risk because the results might be exciting. Shmata did not agree. He claimed that boys learned by doing, and that adventures like this were what gave them character. Besides, young Sammy would be safe because he was in the company of two adults.

"How can you know that?" said Bertha. "How can you possibly know that? Why not just go to Earl's bedside and ask him if the coins are down there? Or would that be too simple?"

These words of Bertha's were bouncing off the windows of Shmata's car when they pulled up in front of the Belanger house. Sammy was sitting on the doorstep, holding a plastic shopping bag. Shmata's greatest hope was that one of the items in the bag would be a flashlight with good batteries. He had forgotten his own.

"Well," said Shmata. He couldn't think of a thing to say to Bertha. He was mad at her.

Bertha gave him one of her looks.

With some strict guidelines in place having to do with Sammy's safety, and an I-told-you-so clause waiting in the wings, Bertha finally agreed to go through with Shmata's plan, and for this he was grateful.

Shmata had wanted to reveal as little as possible to Julie Belanger, and he certainly didn't want to get the boy's hopes up or say anything that might encourage him to talk to anyone. *We want to borrow your boy for an evening or two,* is how Shmata had put it. *And he might be late coming home.* Julie was curious, wanted some details, but she was looking very tired. The media people who had swarmed around her house for several weeks had probably taken their toll on Julie. *We need a strong young boy who can do some crawling around in small spaces. He might come home a little dirty. We'll pay him, naturally. Oh, and we'd like you to come along too.*

It might be fun, Shmata added, without conviction.

Julie said she probably would not be coming along, and Shmata hoped secretly that she would stick to that course. He also hoped that Julie would assume that they were going to do their search in the relative safety of Earl Claney's old house.

"Yiz aren't gunna find it, y'know," said Julie, and just like that, the cat was out of the bag. Earl must have told her to forget about finding any coins.

"We just want to try," said Shmata to Julie, and she shrugged, and that was that.

"Is your mother inside, Sammy?" said Bertha.

"My mom can't come with us," said Sammy, climbing into the back seat of Shmata's car. "She's at a new job. What's that thing?"

Sammy was examining a metal bar with a disc at one end, a handle at the other, and what looked like a radio attached to the handle.

"Is it, like, a crutch?"

"No," said Shmata.

"Is it, like, a periscope?"

"It's a metal detector," said Shmata.

"What's it for?" said Sammy.

"Metal," said Shmata.

"I mean what for?" said Sammy.

"You'll see," said Bertha.

"Will it be like submarines?" said Sammy.

"Will what be like submarines?" said Bertha.

"The crawling in small spaces," Sammy replied.

"Are you afraid about this job we're doing, Sammy?" asked Bertha. "Because if—"

"No, I'm not afraid. My mom, she says if it gets scary just pretend you're in a submarine."

"Do you like submarines?" said Bertha.

"I don't *like* submarines, I *love* submarines."

It was supper time when Shmata parked his car out in front of the doomed San. As the sun began to sink closer to the roof of the old facility, they all nibbled away at their suppers from paper bags.

"Oh, hell," Shmata said.

"What's wrong?" said Sammy.

Two men had just strolled from the rear of the old San, and they were pointing at the main building. They seemed to be there for a reason, and Shmata was pretty sure he knew that reason.

"I thought this place was supposed to be deserted," said Bertha.

"Not a minute too soon," said Shmata.

"Whadya mean?" said Sammy.

"Our mission," said Bertha. "We hurried over here tonight because this place is scheduled for the wrecker's ball."

"Is that, like, a dance?" asked Sammy.

"Shh."

They waited in the car while the men talked. Sammy gave them an update on Earl Claney's condition. Apparently he had recovered from his seizure, and the doctors were even talking about the possibility of another operation. In the meantime, if he didn't have another relapse, Earl might be able to return to Julie's place in a week or so.

After a few minutes, Bertha left the car and strolled over to where the men were standing. Shmata could see her talking and smiling. Presently the three of them returned to their vehicles.

When she was inside, Bertha gasped. "Monday! It's supposed to be Monday morning!"

"This Monday?" said Shmata. "It said in the papers that they wouldn't get to it till next week sometime. Jesus."

"What's on Monday?" said Sammy.

"They're starting the demolition early," Bertha said. "It's because of the historical society, Bill. They were going to picket the San. I think they're trying to get the jump on the picketers."

"Who's gonna pick at the san?" asked Sammy.

"You'll see," said Shmata. "Tonight was just going to be a reconnaissance mission."

"What's that?" said Sammy.

"A little snooping," said Shmata.

"A little digging," said Bertha.

"A little exploring," said Shmata.

"That's one of the things you do in a submarine," said Sammy. "Rickonny…"

"Reconnaissance," said Bertha.

Shmata could tell that Sammy liked the word.

When the men had driven away, Bertha and Shmata took Sammy across the grounds of the Sanatorium to the rear of the building. Shmata carried the metal detector, Sammy his shopping bag, and Bertha her spade, some trowels and a flashlight.

"Don't turn around," Shmata whispered to Sammy. "Makes you look guilty. Just assume you belong here. Don't even bother whispering."

"How come you're whispering?" said Sammy.

Bertha put her hand on Sammy's shoulder. She was pointing at one of the metal coverings on the grass. It was about three foot square and shaped like the roof of a belfry.

"Ever seen these things?" she said.

"That's easy," said Sammy. "Those are air vents."

"Right, and underneath these vents," said Shmata, "you'll find a root cellar and some passageways, and we have to pry these things off one at a time, see?"

"They come off easy," said Sammy. "You don't have to pry them."

Sammy went over to the nearest vent, lifted it up and let it fall upside down on the grass.

"How did you know how to do that?" said Bertha.

"Earl showed me," said the boy. "He said if I ever needed to hide in a perfect place where nobody can find me, these here are just right. He says you'd be safe down there. You could breathe okay down there and everything. That's what it's like in a submarine. You can go way down below the surface of the sea and you can *breathe*. You can breathe and you can look through the portholes and see things."

"Did Earl tell you anything else about this place?" asked Shmata.

"We came over here once," said Sammy. "Easter holidays. Mom dropped us off and we walked around. He showed me his house. Do you like Earl?"

"He seems like a nice enough fellow," said Shmata.

"He's my friend," said Sammy.

"Yes," said Bertha, softly.

"Is there anything you might have forgotten to tell me about this place, Sammy?"

"Nope."

The three of them gathered around the square hole and peered down into the darkness.

"I thought there might be a ladder," said Shmata.

Sammy went over to another vent, lifted off the roof, kicked it aside and bent down, squinting. He looked up.

"Nope."

"Try this one," said Bertha.

Sammy lifted the roof and flung it aside.

"Yep," he said. "This one's got a ladder."

"Hurry," said Shmata, "before someone comes snooping around. Get out your flashlight, Sammy."

Shmata mumbled to himself about Monday and wrecking crews and forgetting his goddam flashlight. He replaced the other two vent roofs, and Bertha handed her spade to Sammy and told him to wait. She slowly disappeared down into the earth and then re-appeared. By the way she handled the climbing up and down, Shmata could imagine what she had been like as a girl. He handed her the metal detector.

"How is it down there?" he asked.

"Pretty dark," she said.

Sammy followed Bertha down the hole, gripping his flashlight. Shmata came last. He descended partway down the ladder and replaced the vent over his head.

"Hold that light, one of you," he cried, and descended the rest of the way.

"Slow down, Bill," said Bertha. "We've got the whole night if we need it."

"We'll need it," he said. "I can't believe they want to tear this place down ahead of schedule. I don't see why they have to tear it down at all."

"You sound like my grandfather," said Bertha. "Good Lord. It's like a bloody mineshaft down here."

"It's awesome," said Sammy.

The boy went first and Bertha had to yell at him not to get too far ahead. They caught up to him, and Bertha placed her hands on the boy's shoulders. She kneeled down in front of him.

"Sammy, do you know why we're here?"

"Yeah, reconnaissance."

"Yes," said Bertha. "And we're hoping you can help us."

"I don't know nothin about this place," said Sammy.

"Yes, Sammy," said Shmata, "but maybe you can still help us."

"We're looking for something down here, Sammy," said Bertha. "Something special that Earl might have hidden down here. Do you have any idea what we're looking for, Sammy?"

The boy shrugged.

"We're going to use this metal detector to tell us if there's any silver down here," said Shmata, "and we have to do everything tonight. So it might be hard work." As Bertha held the flash-light, Shmata fiddled with the dials below the screen of the metal detector. It was a loan from Daniel Meiers, his numismatic friend. The metal detector began to purr like an electric kitten.

"This is for silver?" said Sammy. "Are we gunna find silver?"

"Don't get your hopes up," said Bertha.

"Mr. Shmata, are we gunna find silver?"

"If we're lucky."

"Don't get your hopes up," Bertha said once more.

"Let's go this way," said Shmata. "Hold one of those lights in front of me. Good."

He stalked slowly forward, holding the machine at some distance from his body, because he didn't quite trust it. He looked up and was reassured to see that the passage way was nicely framed with beams and boards overhead. They came to a curve in the cellar, then a wide fork. They all went to the left, and their passageway began to narrow. It terminated in a tunnel at their feet, with a large rusty pipe lying along the bottom.

"Have a look in there," Shmata asked to Sammy.

"That looks just right," whispered Bertha.

"I don't know," said Shmata. "It seems awful damp along that pipe."

"I've got a feeling about this tunnel," said Bertha.

"Is that where the silver's at?" asked Sammy.

"Let's see," said Bertha. "Be careful, Sammy."

The boy squeezed past Shmata and crawled into the low tunnel, straddling the pipe as he went along. He had to swipe the cobwebs away and grunted several times in disgust.

"Use your trowel," said Bertha. "See if there's any sign of digging."

"Are you lookin for that golf bag?" asked Sammy.

"You've heard about it then," said Shmata.

"Because if you're lookin for the golf bag, it's not here. Earl said it got tossed into the river."

"We're not looking for a golf bag."

"What are we lookin for?"

"We don't know," said Bertha.

Sammy crawled out from his little tunnel, flicking cobwebs off his toque and shoulders. He was muttering what might have been swear words.

"Language," said Bertha.

Shmata chuckled.

"I hope you're not afraid of spiders," said Bertha.

"I'm not afraid of spiders," Sammy said. "I just don't like them."

"I'm glad we got that straight," said Bertha.

"You know what I think of when I see spiders?" asked Sammy. "I think of *octopusses*."

They began to look around, sticking close together.

"And you know what I think about when I come down that ladder?" said Sammy. "I think about the *conning tower.*"

They followed Shmata back to the sharp fork in the cellar and took the right-hand passage. It led into a large dank chamber with long spacious wooden shelves on three sides and a wooden walkway leading up and away from the chamber and towards the Sanatorium. Except for a few big preserving jars, the shelves were empty. The root cellar was musty with the smell of ancient potatoes and alkali.

"Look, you two," said Bertha. She was peering up above them at some feeble rays of light. "That must be one of the other air vents."

"Sammy," said Shmata, "give me some light over here."

Shmata and the boy did a sweep of the chamber, walking side by side, up and down, back and forth from end to end, as the machine snored out its monotonous note. Bertha examined the walls of the big room, digging into cracks in the boarding with her trowel.

"There's another room over here," she said.

The machine gave out a little blip.

"What's down there?" said Shmata. "There."

Sammy bent down with his flashlight and pawed the dirt. He came up with a coin. It had a fish on one side and a harp on the other.

"It's just a tiny room," said Bertha. "Filthy, really."

"Is this what we're lookin for?" said Sammy.

"It might be," said Shmata. "Try again."

Sammy grunted down on his hands and knees.

"But it does have some promise," said Bertha. "I've got a feeling about this little room."

"Nothin," said Sammy. "You mean this little coin could make that machine do that noise?"

"That's how it works, Sammy. The coin is probably made of silver."

"Cool," said Sammy.

Bertha had fastened a scarf over her nose and mouth. She looked like a bandit in an old western. She was pulling away at some boards and making her displeasure known to the men outside her newly discovered enclosure. She mumbled into her scarf about lung infections and other diseases that lurked in the alkali, dust and dirt.

Sammy led Shmata over to Bertha.

"Stick your little thing in here," Bertha said.

"It's not a little thing," said Shmata. "It's a big thing."

"Very funny."

"Well, fairly big."

"Over here, Sammy," said Bertha.

"At least I thought so."

Bertha squealed with merriment. Her voice grew very loud and high. Except, when Shmata looked at Bertha under the glare of the flashlight, he realized that Bertha was not laughing.

They all yelled at once.

The metal detector had gone into high hysterics. The closer Shmata held it to the ground in the farthest corner of Bertha's tiny room, the louder it squealed. Sammy was squealing too, and holding his ears.

"Make it stop!" he cried.

"How do I turn this thing off?" asked Shmata.

"How should I know?" cried Bertha.

Shmata finally pulled the detector away from the corner, and Bertha began calling out orders.

"In there!" she cried. "I knew it!"

Sammy stared at her. He was still holding his hands over his ears.

"Dig, Sammy! In there!"

"With this thing?"

"With your shovel!"

"Where's the shovel?" asked Sammy. "I don't see no shovel."

"Well, go and get the shovel!" cried Bertha. "Bill?"

"I don't have the shovel. I'm carrying the metal detector."

"Who's got the shovel?" cried Bertha.

"You have," chortled Sammy, pointing his light at Bertha's arm.

"Oh, so I have."

Sammy went in by himself and Bertha held the light.

"I knew it was in here," she said to Shmata. "I had a feeling about this little chamber."

"Don't get your hopes up," said Shmata.

"Oh, there you go again," said Bertha. "Nothing ventured nothing lost."

"What?"

"You know what I mean."

"I need some light!" cried Sammy.

"Give him some light," said Shmata.

"Go to Hades," Bertha enunciated.

Shmata looked up above him. "I think we've already arrived."

Sammy dug into the dry earth and flung out the dirt. He grunted at the effort of digging, and Bertha and Shmata waited in silence.

"There might be somethin down here," said Sammy. "I think I found somethin."

The boy dug away with renewed fury, gasping and grunting and cursing the dust and the cobwebs.

"Language," said Bertha.

Shmata prevailed upon Sammy to go slower, then to stop digging entirely. With Bertha holding the light, he squeezed in beside the boy and began to paw the dirt away from the excavation. Sammy had found some loose coins, which he put in his pocket, and some fabric, a strong heavy canvas that reminded Shmata of awnings and boyhood circus tents.

"Careful," Bertha muttered.

The boy and the man pawed at the dirt together. Then Bertha handed each one a trowel and warned them once more to go about their digging with care. She sounded like someone muttering to herself on the other side of a partition.

"You don't want to rip the canvas," she mumbled through her scarf.

"I know," Shmata grunted.

He was sweating now, and he and the boy were panting. Shmata tried to lift the canvas from the pit, but he couldn't manage it.

"Oh, boy," Shmata cried.

"What?" said Bertha. "Are you all right?"

"Hey!" said the boy.

"Are you all right?" cried Bertha, lifting her scarf from her mouth.

Shmata reached into the opening of the canvas bag and extracted a smaller bag, also of heavy canvas. He handed the smaller bag to Sammy. It seemed very heavy. Sammy handed the bag to Bertha, and it clunked when she jostled it.

"Holy shit," she gasped.

Shmata climbed up the ladder and eased the tin roof just enough to see. His nostrils were greeted with a waft of sweet summer air. It was getting dark out on the grounds. He hushed Sammy and Bertha, and slowly, like night creatures, they all emerged from below. Sammy fetched the equipment and handed it up to Bertha. Shmata stowed the equipment in his back trunk and returned for the bags. There were six large canvas bags, a leather pouch, a crumpled cigar box, an old Seagram's whiskey pouch, and an old wool hockey sock. The sock and the Seagram's bag were worn and fragile, but the larger canvas bags, though stiffened up with age, had remained strong and resilient in the dry sandy earth. The last item to come up the ladder was the tattered canvas sack that had contained all the other bags. The logo on the bag was just barely legible, *Saskatoon Star-Phoenix.*

"So this is where your friend Earl did his digging a long time ago," said Shmata to the boy.

Joseph Claney had probably done a switch with his younger brother. To fool his pursuers. And if Joe were still alive, he would surely have come for the coins a long time ago.

They decided not to open any of the bags until they were back in the privacy of Shmata's townhouse. Shmata stowed the bags next to the equipment in the trunk of his car, and they drove away. It was a noisy ride home.

THE HOARD

Saskatoon, late May 2003

They walked up the sidewalk to Shmata's townhouse like any family returning from an outing, Mother leading the way. Bertha lugged two canvas sacks as though they were shopping bags. It was dark now, and Bertha didn't see any need to hide anything. Sammy Belanger followed her close behind, carrying two sacks as well, walking with exaggerated nonchalance. Shmata followed them clutching the newspaper sack in one hand and his key in the other. They didn't say a word until they got inside.

They knelt in a triangle on the pale green carpet in Shmata's living room and carefully, one by one, emptied out the contents of their bags for the others to see. The muted murmurs, the *oh wows*, the *looka this ones*, the urgent numismatic questions *(how much is this worth)* slowly gave way to sorting. For a full hour they sorted. The brittle wads of bills were placed on the easy chair, the American silver dollars stacked on the carpet where Shmata knelt, the Canadian fifty-cent pieces piled in front of Sammy. Shmata had to stop gaping, do some relaxed breathing, show Sammy how to hold the coins by the rims, and help Bertha organize the coins according to dates and mint marks. The piles, after fifty-two years, began to reassemble. Fifty-two years. That was one for each card in the deck. Four times thirteen. That was a lot of bad luck.

"What would our friend Letourneau think about this little caper?" Bertha said at last.

"Hell with him," Shmata muttered.

He was looking at the stack of fifty-cent pieces that Sammy was now arranging on the carpet. The boy was very deliberate and almost completely absorbed. To have a son like that, he thought.

"Sammy," he said, "could you divide up all your fifty-cent pieces in two piles for me? One for the Victorians and one for after the Victorians?"

"You mean, like, the guys with the beards?"

Bertha smiled at the boy.

"I already done that," said Sammy. "See? I even divided up the two bearded guys."

"Good work," said Shmata. "Now can you finish lining up the Morgan dollars over here from 1878 to 1921?"

"I thought you wanted to do the American stuff."

"That's okay," said Shmata. "We'll trade places."

"Are you getting tired, Sammy? Because we can take you home right now."

"No, I'm okay."

"What should I do now?" asked Bertha.

She had lines of dirt and dried sweat on her forehead, her hands were filthy, and her hair was all over the place. She looked like a pirate's mistress.

"Place the Peace dollars according to date all in a straight line somewhere. Just like you did with the Canadian silver dollars. Then we can arrange them according to mint mark."

"But what am I looking for?" said Bertha.

"Nothing," he said. "First we arrange them, then we look."

"What for?" said Sammy.

"The good stuff," said Shmata.

"But seriously, Bill. Stop squinting at coins and listen."

He had gone through one of Sammy's stacks of fifty-cent pieces, the Edward the Seventh ones, which went from 1902 to 1910. He was embarking on a second stack, and he was trying to remember something that Daniel Meiers had told him back in February.

"What?" he said to Bertha.

"Seriously," she said. "Bill, if Letourneau finds out about this some day…this hoard of coins, he is going to have something to say about it."

Sammy was staring at him. They were both waiting for him to respond. He looked down at the stack of coins in his hand, and he saw the date 1921. He squinted through his glass to get a better look, and his heart lurched. He slipped the coin into his shirt pocket. *A twennyone.* Isn't that what the man had said at the coin club?

"There's no way Letourneau will ever find out about this," said Shmata, "because I'm not going to tell him. Anyway, he's on extended leave. Besides, this is what they call found money. It can't be traced to any obvious owner, so it's...it's finders keepers."

He rose to his feet, grabbed his magnifying glass, picked up his copy of *Charlton's Standard Catalogue*, and said, "I don't know, Bertha. I think we're in the clear. And I can't think about Letourneau right now."

"Just asking," she said.

While Bertha and Sammy continued sifting through the coins on the rug, Shmata sat by his kitchen table and took out the half dollar. It was a 1921 George V piece, a good strike with very little wear, and it had a ring of green and purple toning around the outside of the coin's reverse and some faint bronze toning on the obverse. Shmata got out his stapler and a two-by-two-inch holder. He stapled the coin inside of this and put it back in his shirt pocket. He looked up the approximate value of the coin in the Charlton guide. His heart was racing.

"Sammy?" said Shmata. "Could you let me see what you've got there?"

"Just about finished," he said.

Shmata turned to the Canadian silver dollars on the carpet. He tried an experiment. If this hoard was as rich as he hoped it might be, he would find a 1948 with no trouble. His fingers followed the silver dollars up from 1935, and there they were: a little stack of Canadian 1948s.

"I don't believe it," he said.

"What?"

"Believe what?"

"You finished over there, Sammy?" he said.

"Yeah."

Sammy was peering at him with the same quizzical look that was on Bertha's face. He had to calm down, he had to slow down. He was getting confused. This was supposed to be an adventure, it was supposed to be fun. But all he could think about was cherry-picking this amazing hoard. He needed a bag to put the best coins in. He knelt among the bags scattered on the rug and found one a little less worn and filthy than the others. It had a draw-string and some lettering on the bottom: *Retourner a Monnaie Royale Canadienne*. He placed the stapled-up 1921 and the four 1948s inside. He cherrypicked some fifty-cent pieces and found seven beautiful Victorians and a stunning 1904. He crawled over to the Peace dollars and quickly found a nice 1928.

"You see?" he said to Sammy. "This big pile of coins has what we call key dates."

"Yeah?" said Sammy.

"So?" said Bertha.

"These key dates are the rare ones," said Shmata, and crawled his way over to the Morgan dollars. "This means that someone…"

"Someone?" said Bertha.

"Let's say it was Bishop Montgomery's father who owned these coins. That's what Willie Grussen said. The father must have been a serious collector. Yes, here's another one. See?"

Shmata picked out an 1885 Morgan from Carson City with light brown toning, a bit weathered, but a pretty nice strike all in all.

"You see this?" he said. "You shouldn't find this coin in amongst a bunch of silver dollars that people used for poker chips. But you might find it…"

"In someone's collection?" said Bertha.

"Exactly."

"But if these are valuable collector coins, why are they just loose in a bag? Why aren't they in some sort of…you know."

"An album," said Shmata. "You've got me there. I mean, this is no way to treat rare coins, even back in 1951. But maybe Bishop's father did what a lot of wealthy men did back then. They just tossed their rare coins into a cigar box and hid them away. We may never know."

"But along comes Bishop," said Bertha, ever the local historian. "He needs some cash, the coins look like ordinary silver dollars to him…"

"The kind they used in their poker games," said Shmata.

Sammy yawned.

"Bill, do you think that these coins would have been worth some real money back in 1951?"

"Yes," he said, returning to the long line of Morgan dollars stretched out before him like a parade of toy soldiers.

"Well," Bertha continued, "perhaps that explains why our departed friends Spencer and Montgomery didn't report their losses to the police. And why Bulger came along to help fetch them."

Sammy yawned again. He couldn't prevent himself. It was time to take him home. He pulled a few coins from his pocket and slowly stacked them on the rug next to Shmata.

"Earl sure had no use for them guys," said Sammy. "The guys who come after his brother?"

"Bill, for heaven's sake, slow down."

He had just found a coin he was looking for, an 1893 San Francisco Morgan. It had some nice original toning and not many scuff marks. He stapled it into a two by two and moved on. There was a 1994 from Phil—

"Bill, I mean it," she said. "You're sweating, you're puffing."

And on she went. She was right. It was time to slow down. It was time to take Sammy home. His mother would soon be back from her new job. The two or three dozen coins that Shmata had bagged were worth more than any collection he had ever seen. And who should get these coins? Julie for sure. Sammy eventually. But what about Montgomery's heirs?

"Bill, we're leaving!"

"Be right there."

The reason Shmata was sweating and puffing, and walking a line between elation and torture, and soon might explode—this had nothing to do with Julie or Sammy or Montgomery's heirs or anyone else. An impulse he had been suppressing at last bubbled up before him: *What about me?* His dream of returning part-time to the Service, of having a bit more security, that had been dashed a few weeks ago. So the words, the greed words or whatever they were, continued to force their way into his brain: *what about me?*

He scooped up the coins that Sammy had placed at his feet a few minutes ago. They all had the design of the fish and the harp, just like the very first coin Shmata and Sammy had found.

These must have been the ones that Sammy had pocketed just before he dug up the newspaper bag. Shmata checked the dates. They ranged from 1941 to 1969. He rose to his feet to follow Bertha and Sammy, who by now would be waiting in the car.

1969?

He checked the date of the top coin, an Irish ten pence. 1969? A bolt from the darkness seemed to pass through his heart. *1969?* Someone had been down there, someone who had decided not to take the trove of coins away. Earl Claney? But why would he scatter some Irish coins, where someone could find them, and not take the hoard away with him?

He was staring at the hallway when suddenly the face of Bertha intercepted his gaze.

"Bill?"

"Yes?"

"You look like you've seen a ghost."

JULIE'S LUCK

Saskatoon, late May 2003

Julie Belanger took the bus home from her four-to-twelve shift. She was so tired she could scarcely think about anything except having a shower and going to bed. Her new care facility was away out on the edge of town. The woman in charge ran things close to the wire, so she couldn't afford to hire enough girls to do all the necessary work of caring for the old people. Fourteen old gals, no men, full bowel care, the whole deal. And two of the residents were pretty much complete invalids. Julie had to run the laundry, do the dishes, and handle all the ladies on the main floor by herself. Thank God the other girl knew what she was doing. Thank God most of the ladies at this new place were good eaters and good sleepers.

The closer she got to home, the more Julie's thoughts turned to Sammy (on a wild goose chase with Mr. Shmata) and Earl (who might be coming back to Julie's house next week). It made her tired to try and think about both of them. Sammy would be all wound-up, or else discouraged, and she wouldn't get to bed till after he told her all about it. And Sammy would be hungry. Julie tried to remember what food there was in the fridge. Thank God it was Friday.

She unlocked the front door and went inside. There before her were Mr. Shmata and Sammy, and standing behind them, a woman with dirt on her face whom she had never seen before.

"Welcome home, Julie," Shmata chimed.

"Yeah?" she said and looked uneasily over at the woman.

"Julie, this is Bertha."

She followed them into her living room, and in one glance she knew, at least remotely, that her life was about to change. She didn't smile, she didn't chide her son Sammy for being filthy and up too late, she didn't offer to make tea for Bertha and Shmata. She was too tired for any of these things. She was too tired to have her life changed, even if it turned out to be a change for the better. There had already been enough changes in the past while to last half a lifetime. And this new mess all over her house, this looked like trouble.

All three of them were looking expectantly at Julie. On every coffee table and end table, on the kitchen table and counters, were stacks of old coins. On the mantle was a pile of old paper money.

The woman named Bertha stood up to say something to her, but she didn't seem to know where to start. Shmata adjusted an arc lamp that Julie had never seen before. It was clamped onto her coffee table. Finally he spoke.

"Julie, this is a bunch of old coins."

He reached over and snapped on the arc lamp and the coins seemed to wink at her their sly old opulence.

"Your son Sammy has just helped us to find them," he continued, "and…"

Shmata beckoned at the coins on the coffee table, the mantle, the end tables, and in the kitchen all over the counters. He waited for Julie's response.

"Jesus," she whispered.

"You'd better sit down," said Shmata.

"Hey, no kiddin," said Julie.

Shmata sprung to his feet and snatched a pile of coin catalogues off the easy chair, and Julie sat down.

"This is all Earl's stuff," said Julie. "Right?"

"Looks like it," said Shmata.

"You got it from his house?" said Julie.

"No," said Bertha.

"We got it from the old San," cried Sammy, pointing to a strange instrument in the hall. "We had to dig it up from a tunnel. We used this *metal detector*."

"Sammy, you're filthy."

"I found the bag," said Sammy with a shy dreamy smile.

"Well, who does this belong to?" asked Julie. "I mean legally."

This late at night, this tired from her shift, she could smell trouble around almost any corner.

Shmata raised his hand until people stopped babbling. "We think it used to belong to some fellows who lived in Banff. They gambled with it, it got stolen, and the main ones are dead now. These fellows may have been responsible for sicking Cletis Bulger on Joseph Claney. Bulger thought maybe these coins should belong to him."

"But we don't think so," said Bertha, smiling, with her hands clasped together.

This Bertha character was too polite, she thought. It wasn't natural to be that polite.

"No," said Bertha. "We think the lion's share should go to you and Sammy. We think you should keep them, or allow us to sell them for you."

"You mean fence em?"

Suddenly everyone, even Julie, was laughing.

"But I can't do that," said Julie. "They're Earl's. They shouldn't go to me."

"We've thought about that, Julie," said Shmata. "I think we all know that Earl won't have them. He's free to change his mind, of course, but I don't think he will. These coins don't really belong to Earl either, and he knows it. He just hid them for his brother Joseph. Do you think we should give them to the families of the boys who got Joe Claney murdered?"

Julie said, "No, but—"

"To the family of Cletis Bulger?"

Julie said, "Maybe not, but—"

"Suppose Earl's brother Joe were still alive, do you think we should give them to him?"

"But he stole em, right?" said Julie. "Besides he dead."

"How about to Earl's greatest friend and keeper?" said Shmata. "And how about to her son who found them?"

"How bout you guys?" asked Julie. "You done all the work, right? You must of figgered it out before Sammy went with yiz."

"We had a hunch," said Bertha.

"Bertha had a hunch," said Shmata.

"So. Say that Earl won't have them. We split the works, ah?" said Julie.

With some discussion and a reservation or two, they seemed to agree with that.

"We could split er up," Julie said once more. She turned to Shmata. "You know about this stuff?"

"Yes," said Shmata.

"Say I got you to sell these here," she said, picking out several silver dollars from under the arc lamp. "How much would I get for them, ah?"

"I'd have to look them up, but a good guess is…they'd get you more than a thousand dollars."

"For just these five coins? No kiddin."

"But I'd rather sell this one for you," said Shmata. He sprang to his feet and redirected his arc lamp to a small pile of fifty-cent pieces on an end table. He picked out one of them from the pile. It was enclosed by a small cardboard holder with a round plastic window. "Here," he said to Julie. "Have a look at this one."

Julie stooped by the end table and held the coin under the arc light. Shmata handed her a small magnifying glass. She squinted at the coin and realized she wasn't quite so tired as she thought. On one side of the coin was an old king with a beard and a crown. The metal around the edge had turned different colours. On the other side was a wreath of leaves and a crest. It said 1921 on the bottom and had some foreign words around the edge. She tilted the coin in the arc light and caught a glint of brown.

"Is that rust?" she said.

Shmata laughed. "That's what we call toning."

"What am I lookin at here?"

"A lot of coin."

"It's not that old. It says here nineteen twenny-one."

"You'd get about thirty thousand dollars for it. Give or take ten thousand."

"Holy fuckin doodle," said Julie.

"Language!" shouted Sammy.

Julie wandered over to the wooden stand that her porcelain tiger used to perch on. She picked up a silver dollar from a stack. It had an oldfashioned-looking lady, a burly young gal with a pile of hair, and an eagle flapping its wings on the other side. She held it up to the light, and it threw out a weird bouquet of pale green, blue and magenta flashes.

"Mr. Shmata," she said.

"Bill," he said.

"What about this baby?"

Shmata put the glass to it. He checked both sides, then brought it over to the arc lamp and squinted at the coin. There was something about him that she trusted, and she wondered what that might be.

"I could get you a couple of thousand for it."

Julie could only gawk.

"Yiz guys want somethin to celebrate?" she said at last.

"Tea will be fine for me," said Bertha.

"Tea is fine," said Shmata.

"I got a bottle a home-made wine somewheres," said Julie.

"Tea will be fine," said Bertha and exhaled dramatically.

"You know? On the other hand, I could use a nip."

It was well past two in the morning, and Sammy had gone off to bed. His last words to his mother were a plea that he might sleep with the metal detector.

The conversation had fallen to murmurs and whispers, but no one seemed tired enough to go to bed. Julie sat slumped on the sofa next to Bill Shmata, kneading Earl Claney's filthy old sack with her bare feet and holding a magnifying glass in her hand. If Earl was still determined not to have the coins, well, she and Sammy would get the really expensive Canadian ones (*key dates*, they called them), and the dogooders could keep a bunch of American ones (*Morgans*, they called them). That library lady, Bertha, she had been just too damned eager to feel sorry for Julie, and so Julie had put her foot down. A healthy split or nothing. *Oh, Jesus*, she thought. *How do I break the news to Earl that we've had this conversation about his coins?* She looked at the magnifying glass as though she had forgotten she was holding it.

Shmata was droning away at her side.

"We know that Earl wants you to inherit most of his estate, right?"

"Yeah," said Julie with a sigh of pure fatigue.

"It would help if you had it in writing," said Shmata.

"I might just bug him about it the next time I go to the hospital."

"Good. So all we need to do is get these coins to a safe place."

"You think the cops might show up?"

"No, not likely," said Shmata.

He yawned and scratched his chest. He looked over at Bertha. She had finally nodded off.

Julie yawned and Shmata yawned again, and Bertha broke into a gentle snore.

"This is just a bunch of old coins that no one remembers. I think they were waiting for you."

Julie shrugged. She was too tired to keep track of all these facts.

"In the meantime," Shmata said, "the word is mum. If Earl could keep a dark secret for fifty years and more, then you and Sammy and Bertha and me, we can keep the secret too."

"Earl once said them coins was bad luck. That's why he's never told us where to find them. He didn't want me an Sammy to get the bad luck."

"They don't look too bad to me," said Shmata. "If our little secret got out, then you might see some bad luck."

"But what kind of luck was it for them two fellas in Vancouver?" said Julie. "They get theirselves beat to death. And what kind of luck was it for Joe Claney?"

"What was that?" said Bertha. She was sitting up straight in her chair once again.

"What kinda luck for Joe Claney?" said Julie. "These coins, I mean. Makes a person wonder, eh?"

JOE'S LUCK

Banff, August 1951

When the bellmen had gone out for the morning shift, Joe Claney appeared with a golf bag at the entrance to Buena Vista. He hustled up the stairs to the top level, shuffled down the hall, toes out, clownlike, smiling his bitter old smile. He swung the ring of keys with some of his old moxy. He was one breath away from whistling. Just in case, he knocked at the first door, paused. In a Hollywood Irish falsetto he cried out, *Laundry!*

Nothing.

He let himself in just as the old char had done every Sunday. The old char was sick again today. She'd caught a flu bug, and she was snoring her way through the morning with her door half open to allow a nice breeze in from the nearby Lake and the mountains. Claney had been getting up his nerve to bribe her, she seemed disreputable enough, but this was an unexpected bit of luck. Claney left a poppy next to her face on the pillow and reached behind her dentures to pick up her pass key.

In and out. Joe Claney, stealthy as a Leprechan. In and out of the first bellman's room, in and out of the next four rooms he shuffled in his worn-down oxfords. Suzy's research had been pretty thorough. She was Lottie's friend, she didn't like Spencer, she loathed Montgomery, and she was up for some revenge on the whole top floor. She had given Joe some clues about where to look and when to pounce. Halfway down the hall a voice moaned at the sound of his key in the lock. He leapt back from the door, and like an actor in a farce, he listened in a deep crouch. When the moaning ceased, he went on to the next room, cried out *Laundry*, swinging his keys, rattling away at the lock. After five rooms the golf bag was getting heavy. Each time he set it down it clanked impressively.

Presently he emerged from the third last room—or almost did, for he heard a noise next door. Bishy-poo in a towel, easing his bronzed body down to the shower. Claney waited until he heard the sound of water pelting. He didn't want to miss Bishy's room. Bishy was, you might say, kind of special. In a burlesque little tiptoe, Joe hurried into Montgomery's room. The blockhead hadn't even locked it!

This one was a double, which meant that Bishop had plenty of places to hide his loot. In Suzy's view of things, the bellmen were mostly rather predictable, especially Bishop, who not too long ago had been her boyfriend. Most of them used the same kind of bags from the bank to carry their coins in. A day or two before a big poker game they would haul their tips over to the little bank in the Hotel and turn them in for fifty-cent pieces, silver dollars and a few large bills. Willie Grussen would always bring enough for the boys who neglected to get their chips in time for the games, but most of them would bring back their silver in rolls of twenty-five, inside the sturdy bags.

This time, Suzie informed Joe, the boys were having an end-of-season all-nighter. It was supposed to be hush-hush, by invitation only. You didn't get in the door with less than five hundred. Three big tables, all the bellmen, their friends, and some selected stooges. Large bills allowed this time only. So Joe was glad he had waited for so long. The take would be big, and the fellows on the top floor had pretty much forgotten about Joe Claney.

Most of the guys would put their cash in with their socks and underwear in the little bureaus by the windows, or under their mattresses at the lower end, or in with their liquor in the boot closet in the corner of each room.

Ah, but Bishy had stowed his cash on a shelf in his bookcase. His lovely white bag of coins was strategically placed behind a photograph of what looked to be his father, and further obscured by some books. Joe also found a Seagram's bag full of coins and a wool sock full of bills tucked inside Bishop's hiking boots. Jaysus begorrah but life was swell.

The water was still running in the shower. Joe had one room to go, Spencer's. He unlocked the door and hauled his golf bag inside. He walked all around the suite until he spotted the stuffed mink that Spencer had won from him on the train. It was perched on top of a box of English ale. The case was a good hiding place. Except, for some reason, Spencer had laid his empty canvas bank-bag under the mink perched on top of the case of ale, as though it were a comforter. The bag beneath the stuffed animal was like a sign: Coins under here in beer box, please help yourself.

Claney helped himself.

The shower was still running when Claney emerged from Spencer's room, and he shuffled down the hall. As he passed each door he whispered a little goodbye, then turned for a final wave. And spotted Bishop Montgomery in a towel, glaring his way, coming his way. Like a startled varmint, Claney scrambled out the exit door and down the stairway. He heaved his booty onto a golf cart just outside the entrance.

It must have taken Montgomery about a minute to find a pair of bathing trunks and some canvas shoes. He exploded out the door of Buena Vista and chased Claney's dust through the parking lot next to the residence, he chased him down the road past the public parking lot by the creek, he slowed when he saw tourists peering his way, and Claney's golf cart disappeared up the little road to the transportation garage. Montgomery followed, puffing his way up the road. Perhaps he looked like an outdoor exercise fiend who simply happened to prefer running in a pair of bathing trunks and canvas shoes.

Claney gained a good deal on the uphill run to the garage. The station bus was inside as he knew it would be. He waved merrily at the dispatcher, a drinking buddy, who was slumped by the door leading to the grease pit and talking with the mechanic, another drinking buddy. Into the dark cave of the service garage Claney disappeared. He took the golf cart around behind the station bus, leapt out, leaned the golf bag against the side of the bus, and threw a huge tarp over the golf cart. Then he squeezed between the filthy wall and the side of the bus and made his way toward the front. He listened. The mechanic was grunting something to the dispatcher. Good. He walked up to the front of the bus, made a fist, and pounded the little knob on the Grayline emblem. The front door sprang open. He wrestled his golf bag inside, closed the door, and hauled his booty to the back of the bus.

When at last Bishop Montgomery puffed his way up to the garage, the dispatcher was gone, and the mechanic had followed him into the drivers' café for a refill of coffee. Montgomery could, he knew, stroll up to the second floor cafeteria and ask a few questions. But Bulger wouldn't be there for moral support, he was on the Lake Louise run, and really, his bathing trunks were a bit on the skimpy side, and all those bigbellied drivers would look him over like he was some sort of exhibitionist, it was very bad form....

Jogging on the spot by the entrance to the garage, Bishop did a three hundred and sixty degree turn and scanned the trees. Some of the men were lumbering down the stairs from the drivers' quarters and the cafeteria.

That wiley little son of a bitch.

Montgomery trotted back down the road. Before he turned the corner, he thought he heard someone whistle. That's when he thought once more of Bulger.

Cletis Bulger is the farthest thing from Joe Claney's thoughts. Joe is in the station bus, up front, gabbing with Milton Corny as the bus descends to the station. Everyone at the Hosh knows Milton, a rotund bachelor as innocent and Christian as they come. Two hotel guests are sitting together halfway down the aisle, on their way to the station, laughing at something and having a fine day.

"Where are you off to?" asked Milton.

"Thought I'd play a few rounds," says Joe.

"You got any golf clubs in that bag?"

"I got the short kind," Joe says.

"Seriously? You takin up the golfin?" says Milton. "I never figured you for the golfin type."

"To tell the truth, Milton, I'm bound for Saskatoon."

Joe wonders if he shouldn't just keep his mouth shut, but who would Milton ever talk to?

"Was at you left one a them new golf carts in the garage?" Milton says.

"No, not me," says Joe.

"Left it under a big tarpaulin? Who the heck woulda done that, eh? Ol Ronnie's out there toolin it around the garage. Drives real nice, like one a them dodgem cars at the Ex? Ronnie says we should keep it, let anybody use it."

Joe says, "Yeah, that's a swell idea, Milt."

Milton says, "I dunno, Joe. Good way to get a mountie at your door if you ast me."

Yeah, the old cop at the door. The old boot in the arse. Life was full of that stuff. Pain and sorrow, sorrow and pain. Fate throws you a bad curve. There might be a bad curve or two for Joe Claney, well he knew. They might sic the cops on his tail, and he might just want to hide out for a while. If they caught him, he'd tell the cops about their crooked games. Big scandal. But right now, with the jack-pines sailing past the station bus and the mountains posing for postcards, and the guesties behind him yuckin it up, and Bishy-poo all in a dither, and all that free cash clunking away at the back of the station bus, right now Joe Claney is feeling mighty lucky.

"I ast those guys back there, I says you guys missin a automatic golf cart?"

Joe looks back at the guesties.

"Oh, Jaysus H. Christ."

"What?" says Milton.

"Don't you know who those jaspers are?"

"Nope."

"Milt, gimme your pencil. Quick."

Milton takes his pencil from behind his ear. Joe looks around and snatches up a golf scorecard from the floor.

"Jaysus, Jaysus, I do not believe this."

"What?" says Milton. "What don't you believe?"

"Just keep yer eyes on the road, Milt."

Joe Claney does his toes-out lep walk down the aisle until he is looking down on the two happy travellers. He is grinning ear to ear.

"Beg yer pardon," he says. "Hate to bother yiz."

Joe thrusts the card and the pencil at them.

"Hiya, sport," says the Irish-looking one, the singer.

The other one, the funny one, says, "If I sign this thing do I get to keep it?"

"Oh," says the singer, "you are such a cutup."

"No," says the funny one, "I hear my autographs are worth a few bucks these days."

"I seen you guys together in three different movies," says Joe Claney. "They're great, them road movies. They're the cat's pajamas."

"Here ya go, sport," says the singer.

"I cannot believe my luck. Hey, whadyou guys think about Mario Lanza, eh? You ever met him?"

"Who's he?" says the funny one.

"You know him," says the singer. "I gave him singin lessons."

Clinging to his scorecard, Joe Claney laughs his guts out all the way back to the front of the bus. *Boy*, he thinks. *When you're on, you're on. Wait till Shorty sees this. His eyes will just bug right out.*

All the way home on the train, Joe Claney keeps coming back to the expression on Earl's face. *His eyes,* he says to himself. *They will just bug out.*

THE SCORECARD

Saskatoon, June 2003

Julie had her speech ready. She had been rehearsing it for two days and she continued to refine it as she rode the elevator up to Earl's ward. *This fellow Shmata, it was his idea. I says to him, you're wastin your time, but he takes Sammy and that library woman and off they go. I figure, no harm in tryin, they'll never find it. But Sammy and them two, damn if they didn't find them coins. I nearly swallowed my teeth. I swear, Earl, I had nothin to do with it, I was off doin a shift out in the burbs. I almost wish the city crew would of found it when they demolished the old San.*

The next part was going to be a tough sell, so she had to say the exact right thing or Earl was going to have another episode on the spot. *The thing is, Earl, them coins might of been bad luck for Joe, but...* The doors to the elevator opened ever so slowly and Julie stepped out. *The thing is, Earl, these here coins have come a long way from Banff or wherever, and they they...they don't...* She went up to the nurse who showed visitors in. She had always treated Julie real nice, especially seeing as how Julie wasn't family and that sister of Earl's *was* family. *Earl, the thing is, you got to realize, we got a bird in the hand here...and...*

The nurse smiled as Julie approached.

"How is he?"

"He seems to be holding on okay," said the nurse. "His voice is a little stronger. We took that neck brace off this morning."

With one arm extended, Julie gestured to the entrance of the ward.

"Oh, yes, Julie," the nurse said. "Go right in."

Earl was sitting up in bed. Without his neck brace he looked skinnier than ever, like a big nestling, maybe a young eagle that hadn't fledged out enough to fly. He was fidgeting with his hands in his lap.

"Well well," she said, hesitating behind a metal chair. "You look ready for action."

"I'm down to my fightin weight."

"They treatin you good?"

"Wish them nurses would stop flirtin with me. They think I'm Elvis or somethin. Might forget myself."

"Earl, I got something," she began. "Something real—"

"Siddown," he said.

She kept her eyes fixed on the metal chair, pulling it out from the bed, perching on the edge of it, adjusting it snug with the backs of her knees. She looked up just enough to see Earl's restless hands, fiddling with something.

"What's that you got?" she said.

"Valentine from a real hot momma."

She made herself look him in the eyes.

"Earl—"

"Before you say anythin, Julie," he whispered, "give me a minute. I got somethin to show ya and I don't want no inneruptions." He took a breath and waved a piece of paper in front of his chest. "I been thinkin about them coins. Hold on, let me speak. They aren't doin nobody no good down there. They might be worth some serious cash. So I was thinkin, mebbe you should just go fetch em and give em to Sammy. Or sell em or whatever. Take a holiday to Vegas."

Julie couldn't think of a word to say. Her speech was becoming unravelled. She made herself wait long enough to think.

"Earl, are you sure? I thought they were supposed to be bad luck."

"If them coins were taken from some fella, mebbe they are bad luck." Earl was holding his piece of paper in both hands like it was a speech he was about to give. "But what if they're given? I mean outright, just given, the way Joey wanted to give them to me. I don't see no harm in that."

"What's in that valentine of yours?"

He beckoned her to approach him and took one of her hands, pressed the paper into it and held her hand closed. "It's a map of how to find them coins," he whispered. "Near my house, down at the San, in the root cellar."

"Oh, Earl," she whispered and felt the coolness and the pressure of his bony hand.

"You'll need help," he said. "Might be a cave-in or somethin. You can't trust them old root cellars."

"Earl," she said, and they were holding hands, and she didn't know what to say.

After a few minutes she released his hand, and there before her was his old golf scorecard with the faded autographs. He had scrawled a rough map on the reverse of the card.

"They're goin to do the surgery," he said.

She raised her head and looked at him and marvelled at the spark in his bloodshot blue eyes.

"What, right away?"

"Real soon. They found a shadow type a deal down here somewheres on the X-ray." He waggled his hand over his torso. "Might be the mother lode. Just, you know, reconnaissance."

"They call it exploratory surgery, Earl."

"Me an Sammy, we like to call it reconnaissance."

"Sammy's been here? He didn't tell me. When did Sam—"

"Yesterday. He come up here and I give him my last..."

Earl toned it down once more to a whisper. "I give him my will. Told him to keep it for you, mum's the word."

"When is this reconnaissance takin place?"

"Doc says I'm strong enough. Probly in three days. They want to take another snip at that thing in my head too. Mebbe same day as the...other. So you promise me, Julie, you won't just go truckin down there by yourself in that there root cellar?"

"Earl, I'm just curious," she began.

She had to say it just right, get this off her chest without revealing too much. After all, she didn't want to give Earl a conniption. Mr. Shmata had told her about a few coins that someone else had left there. Sammy had found them just stuffed under the boards where the big sack was buried. Someone had scattered them around in there quite a few years after Joe was thrown into the river.

"Earl, did you ever go down there to see if the coins was... you know..."

"Still there? Why?"

"Sammy said you took him there once. To the San? To look at them air vents?"

"Did I ever climb down there to check up on things? Why would I go an do that? Place gives me the creeps."

Earl's bloodshot eyes jerked up, and suddenly he was looking over her head. Julie turned around in her chair. A tall pale man with a bony face and a chart was standing over them. Maybe even Mr.

Reconnaissance himself. She sighed. Well, Julie Belanger could take a hint.

She left them together, Earl and the Doctor, conferring and joking and mapping out strategies, the way men do when death is hanging about.

Julie glanced at the scorecard. It had worn thin and wrinkled like the skin on Earl's hands. The autographs were so faded that only an expert with a magnifying glass could tell what was written there. The map on the back was just as iffy. Good thing she didn't need it. Julie tucked it into her purse. If nothing else, it made a good valentine.